Sin City Kilts

BLOOD OF FIRE

JANUARY BAIN

Blood of Fire
ISBN # 978-1-80250-548-1
©Copyright January Bain 2023
Cover Art by Kelly Martin ©Copyright June 2023
Interior text design by Claire Siemaszkiewicz
Totally Bound Publishing

BLOOD OF FIRE

Dedication

A thank you is hardly enough for all the help along my journey, but it's all I have to offer those amazing human beings who have blessed my life.

My incredible editor, Rebecca Baker, who makes my stories so much better and deeper, my publisher, Rebecca Scott, for her continued belief in my work, the owner of Totally Bound, Claire Siemaszkiewicz, for her helpful insights, and my wonderful husband, Don, who makes each day brighter with his humor, support, and unconditional love.

This may or may not be the last werewolf series I write, but I am so grateful for the rollercoaster journey of discovery. Billionaire werewolves are a tough bunch to tell stories about, being rather volatile, you understand, but their antics while finding their Forever Mates are exhilarating and emotional on levels I didn't realize existed until I entered their realm. Thank you, dear reader, for taking the journey with me and blessing me with your time.

Chapter One

Logan

"Bloody feathered tyrant!" I howled at the boisterous sounds of a rooster crowing to greet the morn before the sun was even up tearing through my wet dream like a true cock blocker. *And just when the lass was about to reveal all those luscious curves.* I yawned and checked the clock. I'd best get at it—I did have a lot on before leaving tomorrow. *Directing a movie.* My first full-length feature in Vegas, Nevada, USA. It didn't get any better than that.

I threw the covers off and made my way to the window to pull aside the drapes and check the weather. A half-moon hung smiling in the sky on its way to harvest brightness in a couple of months, the horizon growing subtly lighter to the east. *No fog this morning— the sky clear around the moon.* The distinctive sound of a church bell ringing filled my head, and I shook it in annoyance. Omens I could well do without. Nothing was going to get in my way of achieving success in my own right, not even a seer promising big life changes when I left the Highlands.

Was I taking a chance setting the movie in Vegas, even though it was the perfect location for a heist picture? Both of my older brothers were settled down happily with their new partners and lovers after returning from the City of Sin, acting too smug for words. I shook my head. *No. Not going to happen.* I wasn't one bit superstitious, was blessed with a strong mind and besides, I didn't believe in the thunderclap, at least not for me.

My brothers had just used the excuse to be with the women they wanted to be with. That old crone who'd foretold us all finding our Forever Mates in the land of desert and sage had been full of it. If she could really tell the future, she'd have won the lottery. My philosophy was to live each day to its fullest because it could be the last. *Oh, and protect your heart.*

As a wolf, I'd seen what happened to a shifter who believed in the phenomenon and was rejected by his fated mate, and it wasn't pretty. A passion that raged out of control like wildfire could only lead to one conclusion if it wasn't shared by both.

Death.

Okay, enough drama for one day. It was time to get my mind onto pleasanter occupations. I raced down the stairs two at a time, headed out for a morning run. This might be my only chance for a while. Then I should check in with Finn, my liaison in America. Finally, the farewell party planned for later. That should prove fun—a chance to let off steam before leaving Scotland.

These past few weeks I had been working harder than anyone realized, preparing to take up the reins of directorship as soon as my feet hit the ground in Nevada. I'd prove to them all that there was more to me than the playboy tag I'd been given, though there was much truth to it as well—no apologies for my sexual appetites that were as big as my...caber.

Being naked, I shifted easily, seeing myself in my mind's eye as wolf in the dimension parallel to ours, experiencing a whirlwind of incredible changes as all my energy shifted into a new form, then bouncing back into the normal world on four powerful limbs capable of great feats. That rush—that incredible sensation of letting go then acquiring incredible power—never got old.

I set off, following the trail of prey right down to the water's edge at Creig Loch, where I stood on the shoreline and looked across the deep channel. The rising sun's rays were reflected back to the heavens in a swirling mist of rainbow colors as it advanced over the edge of the world. I could only imagine capturing this on film, what a wolf sees, but it was strictly forbidden. Rule number one was never, under any circumstances, expose your pack to the human world. But it was a shame that humans weren't party to the awesomeness of the universe with blinders off.

The use of light in movie making—that was a favorite subject of mine. More particularly backlight, one of the oldest and most frequently used ways of making people look more beautiful. When focused from behind the actor or actress, making it of greater intensity than the beam hitting the actor's face, it made the subject so beautiful.

Backlit. Like walking through the woods toward a setting sun, when all the world appeared aglow. It was what made Dietrich, Garbo, Marilyn—all of them—even more glorious than they already were. It was what I intended to make good use of in my movie. What was wrong with making the world a more beautiful place?

The chase across the landscape through the glorious scented heather and moss filled me with satisfaction, reminded me of the miracle of creation and renewed my sense of commitment to my ancestors. I was more determined than ever when I turned back toward the castle for the video call with Finn, vowing to make a name for myself, come hell or high water.

* * * *

The day passed at the speed of sound and it seemed only minutes later that I was surrounded by the boisterous late-night crowd gathered in the Creigman's pub for my farewell party. I slipped a large denomination bill from my sporran and, with a wicked smile to the barman, handed the money to him to hold.

"Five hundred to the man or woman who can outdo that performance" — I nodded at the girls dancing to the music, enjoying the evening and wanting to spur on more dancing and drinking until the sun came up — "and a part in my upcoming movie as the stripper in the bar scene!"

Hoots of laughter and wild cheers erupted as the live band changed tunes to *You Can Leave Your Hat On* by Joe Cocker, a perennial favorite at the Creigman's, *the* hangout for weres in Scotland, and the perfect music for the challenge. Hell, I might even use it in *The Vegas Job,* the heist movie I was itching to direct. A well-built blue-eyed blonde was taking center stage. I'd be a hero to all the males in attendance for this one.

Does it get any better? No. I loved my life and all the perks that came with being a billionaire and a shifter. *Who wouldn't?* I had carte blanche to savor all the finer things and pursue my dreams of becoming a world-class movie director.

Sure, I love being an uncle to Lachlan's and Esme's year-old son and looked forward to him being grown enough to throw a ball with, but I wasn't ready to settle down. Sure, one day I might find the perfect woman for me, but right now my art was my focus, and if that meant nights of loneliness I would never admit to unless someone put a gun to my head, well, wasn't that what all the greats suffered to create their own vision of things?

My thoughts were interrupted by a loud chorus of "Take it off! Take it all off!"

The blonde had the crowd eating out of the palm of her hand, holding an untied bra to her chest and gyrating to the sexy beat that made the world drop away. *Now we're talking.* I loved women's bodies, with all those delicious curves. Why did they diet so much when it was curves a man craved?

Halleluiah. The blonde dropped her top and a fine pair of full breasts were revealed. The kind a man wanted to caress and kiss and suck until she was ready for a night of pleasure that ended only when the sun came up and work called. I prided myself on being a generous lover, a charming wolf who made sure my woman got off first.

"Hey, Logan, how about two for the price of one?" Ayla, one of a pair of identical twins that every man worth his salt wanted to bed, asked. She and her twin, Aileen, jumped to their feet, their ample breasts bouncing, making the current champion glare in their direction. But yeah, twin strippers in my movie…that would be hot as hades.

"Sure, give it a go, sweethearts," I said, jerking my thumb at the stage.

My cell phone rang and I glanced at the number. *Damn it.* Just when I was totally enjoying myself.

Tomorrow was soon enough to put on my serious hat and get down to business.

"Logan." I had to shout into the phone to be heard over the whistles and cheers erupting from the crowd. I wasn't the only lover of fine women in attendance.

"Mr. Creig, Finn here. Just letting you know we've found an Egyptian antiquities expert for your film."

"Good. Set up an interview for him on Sunday."

We needed the serious authority that having an expert on the subject could bring to the movie. Hopefully, he was some stuffy old geezer who would look down his bifocals at everyone—well, except me of course—and play the part well, with patches on the elbows of his out-of-date plaid jacket. That at least would save me some precious time dealing with the artifacts and preparing them for display. The complicated setting in a working casino would be ample enough challenge for the foreseeable future.

"Ah, sir, it's a woman. Comes highly recommended, I might add."

"That's all I ask." I revised the image in my mind's eyes to a middle-aged female wearing oxfords and tweed, with serious-librarian glasses perched on her nose. *Good.* As long as she came properly qualified and added a serious demeanor to my movie, she could wear any old drab outfit she wanted. It would just make it that much easier to leave her alone. I might not be superstitious, but I wasn't going to take any chances in the land of desert and sage...even if I'd admit to it out loud.

I glanced back at the twins who had taken the dance to the next level, bumping and grinding against each other with complete abandon. They were too beautiful for words—backlighting was certainly not necessary for this scene.

"Okay, ladies, you both got the part," I announced. "There'll be space set aside for you on the plane tomorrow."

I endured the squeals and shouts of glee that my words caused. Well, a man or wolf had to do what he could to keep the fairer sex happy. It must have been encoded in our DNA or maybe in our hearts, though more likely in our...*cabers* that always wanted to procreate.

Yeah, sure, someday a houseful of little Creigs running around would be great—not like I couldn't afford it. But that was a long way off in the future when I had established a successful track record in the movie business. My instincts had told me to avoid the trap of surrounding myself with women in Vegas, so I knew I wouldn't get together permanently with anyone. No, I'd treat them like the twins I'd just hired...just in case of the slim chance that the legend was true.

Yes, I was all set, I thought smugly, sitting back in my chair.

A wolf with a plan was unbeatable.

Chapter Two

Justine

I took a deep breath, adjusted my reading glasses and glanced around at the rapt attention of all the eager freshmen, savoring the moment as I prepared to launch into my speech on the legitimacy of the curses often associated with Egyptian artifacts. This was the most deliciously fun section of the course I taught at the University of Vegas each semester. That the debate would be lively was guaranteed, but my innate skepticism and well-honed ability to stamp out even a hint of superstitious nonsense would lead them down the true path in no time.

Curses.

They were something I knew all too well. Didn't my mother curse the day my father abandoned us for greener pastures? But far as I knew, he was alive and well and living with his second or maybe his third family in Ohio. Handsome, charming men were all alike, thinking females were easily acquired, then just as easily sloughed off when they developed a wrinkle or added a pound or two.

That was never going to happen to me because my life was all about teaching and writing research papers and creating a circle of friends that guaranteed I wouldn't ever be lonely. If sometimes I secretly envied when a man and a woman found true love, well, I was better off living with never having had my heart broken.

Falling in love and losing oneself in another sounded like hokum to me, and a waste of energy that could be better spent elsewhere. Like in front of an eager group of young minds, looking for answers to things that were quantifiable and helping them obtain degrees. My biggest hope was leading some of them toward acquiring a teaching degree, a guarantee of a brighter future for all.

"Have any of you heard of Tutankhamun's Curse?" I asked with a crook of one eyebrow.

A few tentative hands were raised. No one wanted to be the one who admitted to knowing or believing in such things. That was a good thing and one they'd be rewarded for in life.

"It was reported at the time that there was a warning on Tutankhamun's tomb that read, 'Death shall approach on rapid wings to him who disrupts the King's tranquility.' When Egyptologist Lord Carnarvon and discoverer Howard Carter decided to open the tomb in 1922, they ignored the curse," I began.

"The facts of the case are that Lord Carnarvon, the team's financial sponsor, died four months after the tomb was opened. What's more remarkable is that he died of a mosquito bite on his cheek, and all the lights in his house mysteriously went out when he died. Whether the lights dimmed in reality is anybody's guess. 'Electricity guaranteed' is not enshrined in the Bill of Rights." I shrugged as I made the small joke to a few titters from the audience. "But his death was duly recorded and led to much speculation and belief in the curse shortly thereafter."

A hand shot up. Ah, now they were duly engaged. I loved to influence young minds, get them thinking, then bring them out the other side better informed and questioning everything. That was my job in a nutshell.

"Yes, go ahead," I encouraged the young female student who'd impressed me with her knowledgeable paper on the cultural aspects of antiquities leaving Egypt. She'd debated the right of museums to sell those they held legal provenance to, citing a number of important cases.

"But it was considered a hoax, right, Professor Bell? The paper with the curse written on it was never discovered. That fact was added later to make it seem more real."

"True. But curses can be unleashed in a number of real ways. Think of the bacteria that such a tomb might contain. That's far more likely than a mummy coming after anyone in the dead of night. Or, if you will allow me the luxury of a segue, an artifact of supernatural origin ever being found, like the remains of a spacecraft visiting Earth eons ago — Chariots of the Gods aside."

"Right, that would make sense, about bacteria," the young woman said, rushing to answer. "But I also read something about one in the tomb of Khentika Ikhekhi from the sixth dynasty that contained an inscription 'As for all men who shall enter this my tomb...impure...there will be judgment...an end shall be made for him...I shall seize his neck like a bird...I shall cast the fear of myself into him'."

Some of the class visibly shuddered.

"Good example, Tori. Unfortunately, worries over such curses have caused some mummies to be lost at sea when sailors grew suspicious of why certain things onboard were happening—even though they could be explained scientifically by today's standards—and threw them overboard. Such a terrible waste," I said with a slow shake of my head. "Believing in curses is a double-edged sword. Humans are so often naturally superstitious and it's far easier to blame a curse for bad luck than it is to find the correct answer. Egyptian curses are mostly a cultural phenomenon. The only thing to fear is a disease they might contain over a mummy coming to life to choke the life out of the person it blames for being disturbed."

A few nervous titters sounded. I blamed movies that glorified such shenanigans. All I could do was stamp out ignorance one small fire at a time.

"Now, I want each of you to investigate a historical event or artifact that was found in Egypt that led to the mention of a curse or not in the time of the Pharaohs and report on it for your midterm papers. Dig up all the facts and explain your theory as to why it evolved the way it did. In other words, why it led to the object being labeled cursed or why it didn't happen. That leaves the field wide open for all of you. It will give you the opportunity to really study one artifact and follow its trail from ancient times to where it resides today. Bonus marks if you can discover any object that vanished from the Valley of the Kings into the hands of a private collector." I shook my head.

"So many cultural antiquities have been lost during the time before strong laws were enacted to prevent such things. Tombs ravaged and pillaged without any regard or respect. The least we can do now is try to report on it as best we can. Have a good day."

The buzzer sounded and the students began packing up to leave. Some would dawdle, no doubt, and I waited for the inevitable questions about the newly assigned paper. I was in no hurry. This was where I was most needed, and I loved my job.

"Ms. Bell, could I have a word, please?" Dean Thornton asked, approaching my podium. The students that still lingered stepped back, and I gave them an apologetic smile.

"I'll be back in my office shortly and anyone who has questions can meet me there," I said, reassuring them. My heart rate jacked up. It wasn't often the dean of the university stopped by to see me. A busy man seldom seen in a classroom, he was far more likely to be hitting the social circuit to highlight what was being showcased this year for research grants. I was generally off his radar, being far too consumed by my daily coursework and keeping students engaged to have time to become popular at social events. *Best to leave that to the social climbers and those that want to hobnob with the rich.*

I turned my full attention on the short, middle-aged, balding dean who had a thing for bow ties. I had a theory about bow ties — never trust anyone who wears one. All my experiences to date had proven the theory true more times than not. But a queasy sensation set in that my being up for tenure this year was what was about to be discussed.

"What can I do for you, Dean Thornton?" I asked, giving him my brightest smile. My track record with students spoke for itself. My classes were crowded each year and I was darn proud of that fact. But grant money was another thing, and so far, I had been turned down on all my proposals. Still, research papers were in the bank and I was also promising a book release next year. Surely that was enough?

"How's that book on Egyptian antiquities coming along? Still on target for spring of 2024?" he inquired.

I nodded eagerly. "Excellent, yes, right on track, thank you for asking."

"Good, good." Some of the students and professors called him Dean Two-times. He had a habit of saying some things twice.

"Something exciting has come up, very exciting indeed, and I immediately thought of you." He rocked back on his heels.

Unease coiled in my stomach. What was he going to ask of me? *Please let it be something I can manage in the little bit of downtime I have at my disposal.*

I nodded for him to continue, my face beginning to ache from smiling so much. To his credit, Dean Thornton was grinning just as widely, like he had a delicious secret to share.

"It's come to my attention that an important movie is going to be filmed in Vegas and they have need of a consultant who is knowledgeable in Egyptian antiquities! To the point they would like that special someone to become involved with set dressing to add authenticity and gravity to the movie. And the director is a billionaire, *a billionaire,* who will pay well to have such a person at his disposal. It's early negotiations, of course, but I think we can safely say that money will be no object." He beamed, his smile stretching even wider.

Darn it. That didn't sound like something I could deflect by stressing that midterms would need all my time and dedication. But a movie! And a billionaire directing it? This idea sounded cursed already. I couldn't even begin to imagine being at the whim of a smug, self-aggrandizing billionaire. *Just shoot me now.*

I scrambled to think. "While I'm flattered, I'm certain that any one of the professors in our history department would jump at this amazing opportunity." *Please don't strike me down for my fudging the truth.* "Professor Davidson has seniority over me—he'd be perfect for the position. Didn't he spend his sabbatical in Egypt last year?"

"He's unavailable. And he's not in any physical condition to keep up with what this position entails, while you are well known for your fondness for marathon running. I must think about taking that up one day." He patted his rotund stomach with satisfaction. Did I fail to mention the dean was as wide as he was tall? "My wife has a fondness for the culinary arts. I might even join you for a run one day."

Run with the dean of the university? *Strike me mute now.*

"So, here's the date, time and address of your interview with Logan Creig at the Glitter Palace Casino." He pushed a piece of paper my way. Damp and clammy from the dean's fingers, it was all I could do not to drop it on the tiled floor as I glanced at the typewritten page.

Like some short men with a Napoleon complex, he strutted from the room, obviously considering the matter dealt with. With my usual appreciation for being backed into a corner, I gave a silent scream to the heavens and promised myself an extra-long run this weekend as a reward. Then I groaned, realizing the interview with this Logan Creig was on Sunday morning, my favorite running time. Now I'd be pressed to fit a session in.

And damn it, I don't need this right now. My resources were stretched this term—more students, a book to finish writing and now why don't we add helping a spoiled movie director to the list?

My cell phone rang and I glanced at the number. Marnie. Just the bestie I wanted to talk to. I needed to vent in the worst way. Get the pissed-off feeling out of my system before I headed to my office and became the always understanding, always knowledgeable, always patient professor everyone expected.

I sighed. Sometimes it was hard to be squeezed into a box of other people's expectations. That was why I ran when I could. Running, just enjoying the sensation of the body effortlessly motoring along, no worries in the world… It could be euphoric, transcendent and life-affirming all in one glorious package. It occasionally happened in the classroom too when a lecture came together, the whole more profound than its parts. But running, that was where it was guaranteed.

"So, are you ready for tomorrow's big event?" Marnie asked without preamble.

Tomorrow was our friend Jane's wedding, and we were both bridesmaids. A lavish affair at the Glitter Palace Casino, which, funny enough, was the same hotel where I had to meet that darn movie director person the next afternoon. But months of planning were now coming down to the wire with the nuptials, though most of the burden had been undertaken by the matron of honor, Jane's sister, Ellen.

"As ready as I'll ever be considering what came down today."

"Tell me what happened."

"The dean's tagged me for something that's going to chew up all my spare time. I just know it. He wants me to be the consultant on a movie set here in Vegas." I said the *m*-word with extreme prejudice.

"Really? Do you need an assistant by any chance?"

21

The enthusiasm in Marnie's voice took me by surprise. If only she had a history degree instead of being a dentist. We'd met at a mixer at university and been best friends ever since. Then I remembered she had a love of theater, and since the movie was entirely different from a roomful of patients, she'd have an interest in the job.

But now it was harder to rant about my wanting to throw away what might be seen as a golden opportunity. *Yeah, sure, if you want to be around the kind of men who probably think they're God's gift to women.* I was in the know about Hollywood like just everyone on the planet in the twenty-first century.

"I wish you could take my place," I tried to say without whining. Didn't manage it.

"Well, I could tag along, carry things for you. No charge either. Ah, better yet, give the cast and crew bright new smiles!"

"And what would Ruger say to that?" Ruger was Marnie's long-time on-again, off-again boyfriend.

This time it was Marnie's turn to sigh dramatically. "He's being such a pill about where we go on vacation this year. I want spas, bars and lying around in the sun and he wants sky diving, mountain climbing and skiing. It's a good thing we're so compatible in bed. But is that enough? When we're out of the sack, we want different things."

"Passion dies at some point," I said with my practical, jaundiced view of human behavior. If I was ever to get together with someone—and that was a huge *if* considering my track record—I wanted that person to be interested in sharing activities. Not everything—that would be weird—but enough to feel like he was my friend, not just my lover.

"Exactly! And if you don't even share some common goals or like to do stuff together, what have you got? Ruger."

"But wasn't he there for you when your grandmother died last year? Insisted on going home with you and taking care of things."

"True. He is good to me about things like that."

"Well, you can't break up now and ruin the pictures! Ellen would pitch a hissy fit unbecoming of the sister of the bride." I reminded her of the other tyrant who had been running the show for months now.

Marnie gave a snort. "Wouldn't want that. Remember the rehearsal dinner and the waiter who forgot to fill the glasses with bubbly for the toast? Capital offense. I thought she'd have him strung from the nearest ship's mast or keelhauled." Marnie's father was a major general with the US military, a fact she was proud of.

"It's going to be so much fun!" I said with an amused shake of my head.

"I'm strapping a flask to my thigh. Only way I'm getting through this."

"Great, make sure there's enough for two. Gotta go. I have students waiting."

"Okay, but be prepared to abandon ship tomorrow."

"*Seas* the day. Act like a lady and curse like a sailor, my friend."

I ended the call to the satisfying sound of Marnie's contagious laughter. Right, one last skimpy meal to make sure I fit in the dress for the event, then I could eat like a normal person again. Why did Jane have to choose such a body-hugging style? Right, because *she* was as thin as a rail and loved to show that off.

I, no matter how much I ran my ass off, still had ample curves. Right then and there I promised myself a serious celebration soon as the ceremony was over and Jane could no longer dictate my actions…

Chapter Three

Logan

"Welcome to the Glitter Palace, Logan Creig." Cristaldo, alpha of the House of Luceres, came forward to greet me and my team in the opulent lobby.

Dressed to the nines in an impeccable dark suit and expensive jewelry, his demeanor professional and yet warm, the owner of the huge casino hotel complex, the biggest in Vegas, was good to have as an ally and friend. We were in an elite league, being werewolf shifters, and sure to have each other's backs.

"Thanks, good to be here." I clapped him on the shoulder, then turned to my crew. "This is the man responsible for making all this possible."

Cristaldo had offered the venue soon as I had approached him with the idea of a heist movie set in Vegas, and I wanted him to know I appreciated the support.

"Anything any one of you needs, just ask," Cristaldo said with aplomb, addressing my team. A tall, dark-haired woman in a conservative suit came up to join him just then and he quickly introduced her. "This is Madelyn Smith, and she'll be the overseer of your stay, working alongside Finn Creig."

"Welcome to the Glitter Palace," she said, nodding at my group and smiling warmly. "Anything you need—"

"I just need a room and a bed. Jet lag's a bitch," Ayla grumbled, interrupting the woman and making her twin sister, Aileen, frown at her.

I doubled down on that disapproval. I hoped I hadn't made a mistake bringing along the twins. Maybe she was still hungover? The pair of them had been knocking back the shots last night at the Creigman's with a great deal of zeal, celebrating their new roles in *The Vegas Job*.

First order of business, I'd make the importance of 'moderation in all things' during a shoot clear to everyone. Oh, and always paying proper respect to an alpha. An email sent to all parties would take care of that. Or maybe an admonishment from their alpha might be in order. I wanted the movie completed without a whiff of scandal. Ultimately, success rested on my shoulders.

"We have an entire floor of rooms booked for everyone. Please, follow me," Madelyn responded, her smile a work in progress.

I nodded at Cristaldo. "I've brought along gifts from my clan to yours. I'll have them brought to you shortly."

"Join me for a drink in Nero's as soon as you've settled in."

I accepted his offer and strode over to the bank of elevators. Using my key card to open a private car, I hit the number for my floor, located one above the others.

I needed privacy during the shoot for my own sanity, with filmmaking being such a tense occupation that demanded a lot of its director. I stood impatiently in the confined space, waiting for it to ascend.

The romantic strains of the theme music of the movie *The Bridges of Madison County* were playing and instantly sent me on a journey to review the brilliant storytelling of one of the great masters, Clint Eastwood. His use of light and sound to capture the magic of an overwhelming instant attraction between a pair of lovers was moviemaking at its finest. That the male lead was also a photographer aided Eastwood's commitment to creating beautifully framed shots.

I chuckled. It would be like a real robbery happening during the shoot of *The Vegas Job*, something I was not advocating for just to add authenticity.

The elevator stopped and I stepped out. The magnificent suite that greeted me was ostentatious, all high-end furnishings exactly right by Vegas standards, but way over the top for my personal needs. But, as they said, image was everything, and looking the part mattered more than anything in an industry that appeared more glamorous than it really was.

The king-sized bed, all plush and ready for action, dominated the huge bedroom I hurried through on my way to shower off the plane ride. I particularly liked the strategically placed amenities like the wall of mirrors and the built-in comforts of liquor and high tech. Everything I needed was already in place, overseen by the incomparable Finn.

As he was also in charge of the gifts to be presented to Cristaldo upon arrival, no doubt he'd be along any minute. He was located on the floor with my team, the man in charge of petty squabbles and the like. *Note to self, give the man a substantial bonus if he has to deal with those twins too often.* My own fault. I hadn't vetted them properly, just made a spur-of-the-moment decision to satisfy the home crowd.

I would have to be careful of that spontaneity going forward. But hell, I was in Sin City, where anything could happen and often did. My blood fired with heat and my cock twitched just thinking of all the gorgeous women who often descended on Vegas.

Eager to rejoin my host for a drink, I took care of the essentials of bathing then re-dressed in an impeccable black designer suit that fit my extra-broad shoulders, corded, muscular biceps and trim waist thanks to an excellent tailor. The choices were vastly different from my usual kilt and white shirt back home, but less noticeable in Vegas, where I had no interest in standing out beyond the simple facts that I was taller than most men at six-four and tied my hair back with a proper leather strap. *Not like I want that to ever change.*

I descended to the lobby and ran into Finn as I strode toward Nero's. He had his cellphone in his hands, busy texting someone. He'd be lucky if he got to put the device down for five minutes during the next six weeks of the shoot.

"Walk and talk," I instructed and he joined me with a quick right turn, matching me step for step.

"Quick update. Everyone's settled in and I've given them instruction to meet you at Nero's for a seven a.m. call on Monday morning. Everyone was pleased they have Sunday to acclimatize," Finn said, his short fire-red hair shining above his perspiring face.

A tall, thin man and very efficient at his job, Finn was all I could ask for in a liaison and overseer of operations. "Also, I took care of having the gifts delivered to the penthouse as soon as you arrived."

"Good man. Has that shipment from Egypt arrived yet?" I'd made a trip to the land of the pharaohs last month and ordered a few large crates of artifacts to be delivered to the casino in time for the movie. But customs could be a bitch and I hoped they wouldn't be held up due to red tape.

He shook his head. "All promised for the morning. Cleared customs yesterday. They're cutting it fine, but saves us needing to store it for long. There's a room set aside on the main floor."

"Okay. Good. Want to join Cristaldo and me for a drink?" I nodded at Nero's as we came to the doorway.

"No. I have a few more things that need finishing up before this head hits the pillow."

"At least take some of Sunday off. You've more than earned it."

"No time. No different from you. You've got appointments and interviews as well. Until the movie's in the can, this will be the norm."

"True. Okay, see you in the morning."

As Finn hurried on his way, I caught a glimpse of what could only be a wedding party moving as a large group toward one of the ballrooms. The bridesmaids took my attention, dressed as they were in silky red gowns that swept over curves and valleys with loving attention, a perfect foil for the golden glitter of the décor and the black of the men's tuxes. At least a half dozen gorgeous females with upswept hairdos and animated expressions dressed up the view.

One in particular drew my eye, a beauty with generous curves, her white-blonde hair like spun silk fastened into a cascade of curls on top of her head with a few loose ones teasing sculpted cheekbones and luscious deep pink lips. *Yes.* She should be in movies.

Or be highlighted as the newest, most beautiful woman for that special yearly edition of *People* magazine.

But even more than that, she had something indefinable that could only be called star power — something one had or did not, and something that could never be learned. A profound energy or charisma that defied words but was easily enough recognized when in its presence. Her fair complexion was lit from within. A scent drifted to me from the overhead air conditioning and I knew it was hers. Roses with a hint of warm female flesh that captivated me. I'd recognize that scent anywhere now.

She turned and spotted me at that moment and my libido took a direct hit. *Yes, she's really something special.* I turned away with reluctance, wishing I could have caught her image on camera.

"You made it. Sit. Are you hungry?" Cristaldo greeted me.

"Famished."

He nodded and the waitress appeared at my side, taking my order for a juicy steak with all the trimmings.

"Everyone settled in all right?" he asked, taking a sip of golden liquor from a heavy-bottomed crystal glass, his dark brown eyes alert, scanning the room as we talked. The alpha had a lot on his plate. He ran an empire worth billions and he ran it well, by all accounts.

I shrugged. "So far. Last thing I need or want is a group of special divas, if I can help it. I might have made a mistake bringing those twins."

"Give it time. They're young. These things usually have a way of sorting themselves out."

"Hope you're right." My steak arrived and I tucked into it.

"How is it?" Cristaldo asked with interest.

"Perfect."

"Do you get a lot of weddings?" I asked nonchalantly after swallowing another delicious bite.

"Weddings, conventions...we host everything. From karaoke to comic cons. Not a week goes by that we're not booked solid. In fact, we've got a wedding this weekend in Dreamland, a live broadcast of a poker convention convened in Sparta's and a spring break pool party that I hired extra security for. We create jobs here and the Nevada State Gaming Commission loves us for it." Cristaldo punctuated his remarks with a sip of his whiskey and a nod. "By the way, your movie is creating a great deal of excitement for everyone involved with tourism."

My heart rate jacked up with anticipation.

"How many visitors does Vegas get a year?" I was imagining the hordes of people that I would need to keep *out* of my shots. Of course, we had a sound stage booked and sets being built for many scenes, and the use of Nero's for some inside shots. And for the sole purpose of authenticity, we were going to use the Cleopatra Room for the actual heist shoot, located just off the main lobby of the Glitter Casino for the display of priceless Egyptian artifacts that the thieves were going to steal.

"Over thirty-two million last year. A hundred and fifty thousand hotel rooms in this town. But don't worry — you'll shoot the robbery itself at night, right? We can block off the area easily enough to keep strays from ruining a shot."

I nodded, finishing my steak and trying the whiskey.

"Dalmore 62? Excellent choice, extra smooth," I said.

"Just the finest single malt whiskey ever produced."

"Don't let The Creig hear you say that. She'll defend the Highland's finest single malt to the death with a duel at dawn. You received the case of Macallan Lalique that Finn delivered, courtesy of our esteemed grandmother?" My solemn expression hid my amusement.

Cristaldo chuckled at my words. "I did. I must thank her for the generous gesture. Shall we say it's a tie and prevent a war?"

"Works for me." My hunger satiated, I leaned back and made a closer inspection of my surroundings. Nero's architecture screamed Roman coliseum, with ornate pillars and life-sized statues strategically situated all around the vast space. The frescoes of the Italian countryside on the walls were a nice homey touch, but the overhead display of a night sky added such depth to the ceiling that it vanished, giving the impression of the outdoors. "I like what you've done with the place," I deadpanned.

"Not too shabby, eh," Cristaldo said with a grin. The Dalmore was loosening him up and we shared a smile over another silent toast with the fine whiskey.

"I want to say how much I appreciate your allowing filming here."

"Mutually satisfactory. We get a plug in your movie. Both of us benefit. What's not to like?" He shrugged.

"Let us know if there's anything we can do for you." Both our clans had sworn to aid the other generations ago, and the call went out from time to time for assistance. In a world of humans, we werewolves stuck together. A united force against not only humans, but other supes, vampires in particular. Eternal enemies were still a thing, though of recent years the animosity had lessened somewhat.

"Always," he said before taking the last gulp of his whiskey. "Another?"

"Thanks, but I'd better not. Got an early morning call."

Cristaldo nodded. "A wise man not to add a hangover to jet lag. I hope the rest of your crew show the same resolve?"

"We'll see. Finn's running herd on them. I wish him good luck with those twins."

We got to our feet and shook hands. "Anything you need, just ask, Logan. I'm here for you. We've got the cast party for the last day of shooting planned as well."

"Good. Thank you for all you've done. It will not be forgotten." I shook his hand to seal the deal.

"We help each other. It's the creed of our kind."

"Yes, our ways are the best."

We took our leave, my host vanishing into the back of Nero's while I decided to tour the ground-floor venues of the casino to get my bearings. Dreamland…where the wedding was being held.

A quick look can't hurt, right?

Chapter Four

Justine

I chanced a glance at the dance floor from my assigned chair, discreetly accepting the seemingly bottomless flask of excellent tequila from Marnie under the white tablecloth for the third time. Married two hours ago, Jane, currently the reigning champion bride from diva hell, had finally calmed down and was at that moment dancing a romantic waltz with her new husband. Maybe we were finally off the hook?

Marnie and I deserved the break. Jane had been even more difficult than expected and that was saying something. I mean, who asks their bridesmaids to hand over their phones, submit to a drug test, tells them to abstain from alcohol and encourages them to look less pretty so the bride will be the most beautiful for her big day?

I kid you not! Actually, she had her mom deliver that news, too busy with her entourage of makeup people to bother with us. We did each other's faces and hair and we still looked good.

I took another swig of the potent liquor that made my blood sing. I was giving myself this one night of decadence. Who cared if I arrived with a hangover for tomorrow's interview? I didn't even want the damn job.

Well, at least my bridesmaid gown was beautiful. Marnie had insisted on them, not letting Jane have all the say on that one thing. She called it payback for having to put up with her sister this past year during all the wedding shenanigans. And, surprisingly, she'd pulled it off. I'm not sure how. Maybe she'd threatened to do something to Jane in her sleep, like draw on her face with permanent marker if she wouldn't relent from the monstrous choice she had originally made that would have better suited Little Bo Peep.

"So, how soon until we can join the main party?" I whispered in Marnie's ear, not wanting to draw the attention of any of the other bridesmaids. *Paid spies, all of them.* I'd discovered that earlier when I had innocently asked what time we were allowed off the grandstand and Jane had chewed me a new one for not being grateful for the honor of being her bridesmaid.

"Soon. Jane wants one more series of photos— though I think she has enough to open her own studio—then we're free to do what we want, as long as we stay in the ballroom. Then we can hit the bar and get all the free drinks our hearts desire."

Marnie leaned in closer, the liquor scenting her breath, but not in a bad way. "You should really think about hooking up with one of the wedding party or a guest. Or that awesome hottie we saw in the hallway earlier. You can't just ignore the time-honored bridesmaid hookup tradition. And isn't it time you put yourself out there? Not all men cheat, you know. And a bit of fun will blow away the last of that awful Brad asshole. You were way too good for him. A one-night stand would be good about now. Heck, don't even exchange names. Keep it all about the bod. Get your groove on, girlfriend. You know it's time you rode the waves, skippered the boat, put up the mainsail. You're not done boating until you're put away wet, but watch out for the boom!"

I laughed at her antics, at Marnie being Marnie. But she had a good point. I had dropped off the dating scene these past months since Brad and I broke up. The man still lived with his mother at thirty-five and had no plans to ever move out. Not that I wanted to marry him, but still, his mother was in darn good shape even though she called him incessantly with even the tiniest of complaints.

Like the time we were celebrating our six-week anniversary at a fancy restaurant and she needed help setting up her newest e-reader. *Grab a paperback for heaven's sake, until we finish our meal at least.* But no, he had to go home and deal with it immediately. In a real emergency, I'd be there in a heartbeat as well, but it wasn't just that. Brad just hadn't been alpha enough. Too milksop by a country mile. Not someone I could call *sir* when things heated up.

"Maybe I might even find someone I can call sir," I teased, thinking of the kind of fun I wouldn't mind exploring, making Marnie's eyes widen with interest and me realize I'd had a bit more to drink than I realized. I'd never let that cat out of the bag before.

"Do share, matey," Marnie quipped back, raising her eyebrows.

I reached up to tuck my hair behind my ears and discovered in horror something missing. "My earring! It's gone."

I looked frantically around, checking my lap and the tablecloth in the vain hope it would magically appear. "My grandmother's. I have to find it." I slid down and crawled under the table, searching around the chair legs and other people's feet. The emerald and gold earrings were the most precious items I owned, given to me by Nana on my twenty-first birthday.

"Maybe it fell off in the bathroom?" Marnie asked, joining in the search. We were both the recipients of a nasty look from Jane as we searched. I ignored her. This was an emergency and I wasn't going to let her stop me looking for the treasured heirloom. Thoughts of losing such a precious gift brought a wash of tears to my eyes.

"I'll be back," I promised and took off at a half-run for the ladies' room. I'd used the one in the hallway earlier instead of the one inside the venue to escape the taxing situation for a few extra minutes, but now I was regretting it. At least in the one in Dreamland I stood a better chance of someone handing it in to lost and found or remembering that they'd seen me wearing them at the ceremony.

I raced through the open doorway, holding my skirts up to avoid tripping and rounded the corner. *Just a few more feet —*

"Where's the fire?" a deep voice asked to my right.

Without looking back, I yelled over my shoulder as I pushed open the bathroom door with both hands, not wanting anyone to think there was an actual fire. "Nothing's burning. I just lost something."

I searched frantically — on the floor, in the sinks then in the stalls. *Nothing.* I tore open the garbage disposal and began throwing out the damp paper willy-nilly. *Again, nothing.* I tied up my mess, washed my hands and stood there, thinking. Maybe it had fallen off in the church? I needed to make a call and find out, but I had no damn phone, thanks to Jane.

I took a moment to compose myself, not liking the hot mess I had become in the past few minutes. I dampened a paper towel with cold water and pressed it to the back of my neck. It helped, just like when I got a migraine. I felt better when I exited the room a few minutes later.

"Ah, the lady who lost something."

I stopped, recognizing the deep voice, annoyed that he was still hanging around. Then I had a better thought—maybe I could borrow his phone? I made a sharp turn—

Oh. That man, the one from the hallway earlier in the evening. My pulse spiked. He stood before me in all his glory. My mind went blank as I drank in his assets. He had all the bases covered. Handsome. Impeccably dressed. An amazing physique. Thick light-brown hair tied back and shining with golden streaks that gleamed in the soft light. But the best part was his emerald-green eyes surrounded by thick dark eyelashes.

Wait! *Emerald*—I was looking for my earring, not a man. A voice spoke inside my head, surprising me. *Isn't this supposed to be your one night of decadence? Why not let go? Give this Adonis a few minutes to see if it leads anywhere?*

The man smiled and my mouth went dry. I swallowed, aware I was appearing star-struck and not happy about it. "Yes, I've lost something very precious, my nana's earring. She gave them to me when I turned twenty-one and now one is missing." Tears came to my eyes that I blinked away, feeling foolish for becoming weepy in front of him.

It had to be the tequila making me so emotional. It was so strange standing there, like I had an instant connection to a complete stranger. Maybe because he was so damn good-looking? Not that *that* was the most important quality I was looking for in a man. No, I wanted intelligence first and a sense of humor was a plus. *Okay, handsome doesn't hurt.*

"I understand — completely. I always wear the St. Christopher's cross that my grandmother gave me and would suffer its loss. Can I help? Where were you earlier this evening?"

Empathy for my predicament was clearly written in his remarkable eyes, making my body hum with a vibration I could only call anticipation of excessive pleasure. "Yes, please. I need to borrow your phone. I was at the church, so maybe it dropped off there?"

Without another word, he pulled the device from his breast pocket, unlocked the home screen and handed it over to me, a complete stranger. But then, what was I going to do? Run from a man who had longer legs than me? Did I mention he was tall, with extra-broad shoulders barely contained in his obviously expensive suit? *Imagine what he would look like naked...*

Gathering my errant thoughts, I hurried to look up the listing for the Guardian Angel Cathedral and called them. Waiting for someone to answer, I checked out the man again, glancing up at him through my own thickened-by-mascara eyelashes. *Impossible not to.* He stood waiting at my side like he was in no rush to leave. He most definitely was the best eye candy I'd ever been exposed to in this lifetime, far better looking than any movie star on the big screen.

And he smelled so good! What was that divine scent? Something expensive, no doubt. Who was he? Did I really want to know? That would just spoil the illusion of this unexpected meeting that had a bit of a serendipitous note to it. Marnie was right. No names, a quick roll in the hay and move on. *Prove I'm over Brad.* Now, I just needed to talk this hot man into it. And ask him to wear a condom. *Safety first.*

"Hello, yes, I'm looking for my earring. Did anyone turn one in to lost and found this afternoon? It's a gold setting with an emerald in the center."

"Sorry. No one has turned in any jewelry or anything at all today," the voice over the phone replied.

"Thanks." I hit End and bit my lip, my spirits dropping.

I handed the phone back and he leaned in closer to me, sending my libido reeling. "Hmm, what do we have here?" he said, his fingers brushing my hair and the side of my neck and making my whole body tingle with anticipation. *Yes.* This was good. *More, please, sir.*

Like he'd just pulled an ace out of thin air, the man dangled the missing earring in front of my disbelieving eyes. For one split second, real magic existed, like he'd reached into the fifth dimension and returned with his gift. "Where was it?" I asked, delighted, reaching for it.

"Stuck in your hair, almost invisible to the naked eye. Please, allow me." He expertly fastened the earring back in place while I stood obediently still. Hell, I didn't want to go anywhere, especially not back to the wedding. Would Marnie understand? *You bet.* However, Jane would disown me and most likely burn me in effigy in the morning. But too much tequila and passion were racing through my bloodstream to care about that.

"Thank you."

"You're welcome, Miss…?"

I pressed my forefinger to his gorgeous lips, the boldest move I'd ever made in my entire life. "No names. Two ships passing in the night looking for a safe harbor."

His eyes lit up, the emerald color becoming so intense that I was mesmerized and couldn't have moved if someone had put a gun to my head and threatened to pull the trigger. Tonight, I was going to be just a woman—not a professor, not a bridesmaid, not a recovering ex, but a woman who wanted a man. And not just any man, but a virtual God of a man in her bed that would prove she wasn't dreaming. Maybe it was the tequila. Maybe it was me. Maybe it was fate. But at this moment, it felt exactly right.

"As you wish, angel. Okay if I call you that?" he asked, leaning in even closer as if breathing me in. His minty breath graced my cheek. I also caught a trace of spirits. He had been drinking too. *Perfect.* For one night to let things go and embrace our inner wild child. But if he saw me as an angel, I wouldn't complain.

"Yes. And I think I'll call you Logan. That's my favorite male name." I intended to call my future son Logan, but I didn't think he'd appreciate hearing that. But the idea just popped into my head for some strange reason, and I couldn't back down now. This was a night for being someone else, someone without limits or that annoying inner voice that always pushed for control, insisting that I was less than the best version of myself and needed to work harder than most to make up the difference.

His eyes widened at my pronouncement. Maybe he didn't like being called by another man's name? But he didn't object, just asked, "Want to have a drink, angel?"

"If that drink's in your room, Logan?" I couldn't believe how brazen I was being. My head spun with it. But hot damn, it felt good to feel free. Yes, raise my mainsail like Marnie suggested and head for the open water. The scent of a fresh breeze stirred my senses, until I realized it most likely wafted from the duct work in the hotel. They pumped oxygen into places like this to keep people alert and gambling. *Or maybe that's an urban legend.*

His eyes smoldered as he took my hand, swallowing it up in an envelope of warmth and electricity. I swear the connection was immediate, like our bodies knew each other. The wedding long forgotten, we swept down the hallway in our own magic bubble and toward the bank of elevators.

When the doors closed behind us in the confined space, he dropped my hand and pulled me close, holding me against his strong, powerful body. Then he was kissing me like he wanted to devour me, his mouth sliding against mine with increasing pressure until my knees went weak with need. My whole body instantly began humming, all my atoms aligning in the most pleasurable of ways. *Yes.*

I should have been concerned—I didn't know this guy from Adam—but I wasn't. It felt ordained. *Exactly right.* And I was lost to its sway. Excited beyond reason, probably due to far too long a dry spell without a man's arms around me...

The elevator door slid smoothly open and the man I knew as Logan picked me up in his strong arms and bore me, light as a feather, to the bedroom. He laid me back against the pillows, his gaze never leaving mine.

"A drink?" he asked.

I shook my head. I wanted this man, and I wanted him now. Any delay and I might lose my nerve. Besides, I'd had enough to drink tonight if I was being honest.

Without preamble, he unzipped my dress and tugged it down off my shoulders along with my strapless bra, exposing my breasts. He pulled the pins from my hair and let the long, fair strands fall down around us as he murmured, "So silky and beautiful, just like you."

I reached up and ran my hands through his hair, untying it as well, allowing the thick locks to loosen and fall in rich waves around his face. Even his hair felt alive, crackling with energy.

He pulled me upward and drew one of my erect nipples into his mouth. He tugged with his lips on my breast, making me squeeze my thighs together to ease the pressure.

I arched my back and pressed myself tight up against him, wanting to be with him more than I had ever imagined possible...but like I'd always thought it should be. A desire to be with a man beyond all reason, like Paris and Helen causing the Trojan War.

For me, it had to be overwhelming—if it was right. Perhaps to assuage the guilt of hooking up? But no, this felt like so much more than that. And for one night only, I would put aside such thoughts and live in this one precious moment of time.

He pulled the rest of my damp clothes from my overheated body. Then I watched as he did the same. A warrior's body emerged, heavy muscles corded under a golden tan, a huge cock proud and ready. The dreamlike state continued as he pressed up against me again, his need for me as obvious as my need for him. His mouth on mine, his hands on my body, so tight that his fingers pressed into my flesh almost painfully. He ravaged my mouth, scalding, tasting of life, and an intoxicating rush of pheromones pulled me into the whirlpool of lust. Liquid flames engulfed me.

"Make love to me, *now*."

"You're killing me, angel. I need protection." He opened the top drawer of the nightstand and grabbed a small box, shaking out a silver-wrapped package. He tore it open with his teeth and rolled it down over his cock. I lay back on the bed and spread my legs for him, enjoying the lust that brightened his eyes even further, their emerald shine visible under the glow of the night light. Like a feral beast's, they made me shiver with anticipation, like we truly were not made of this world, but of a magical realm that defied description.

He came to me then, his massive body looming over mine. He ran his hands all over me until I was trembling with pent-up passion. Caressing, tugging, kissing, treasuring my flesh, nibbling his way down my body, not missing anything. I thrashed my head back and forth on the pillow, my desire to be possessed overcoming any thought of shying away. *One night only.*

I came right off the bed when he ran a finger down my drenched pussy, spreading the quivering lips. Every nerve ending alive, my blood sang with the thrill. He pushed a finger deep inside my channel, into the center of my heat, sending more pleasure zinging through my body. The warmth of his breath teased the sensitive tissues, dancing across my swollen clit and turning me to liquid flame. Every part of me was wide awake, searching, hungry, seething with unbridled lust, the pressure almost too much to bear.

"Please, please, fuck me," I said, the delay an agony, my voice so low and throaty I barely recognized it.

"Not till I taste you, angel."

His words electrified the very air I was breathing.

He pressed his mouth against the juncture of my thighs, hot breath searing, velvet tongue lapping. I let loose wild moans, my body too full of anticipation to keep it all inside. When I could handle no more, I mewled my surrender, driven nearly insane.

"Please, Logan," I whispered, so needy I couldn't imagine existing one more second without release from the unbearable pressure.

He moved, seeming to understand my desperation. Centering himself between my shaking thighs, Logan entered me in one amazing thrust, sending my senses reeling and reaching for climax.

"Oh, sweet heaven above," I moaned, hands firmly planted on his ass, forcing him to push into me as far as possible, wonderful thrusts of pure pleasure over and over until we became one bucking beast…one energy. His cock was so huge I swore we'd never be able to pull apart, until they'd find us one day, still connected. *Pure bliss. And the best fucking sex of my life, bar none*, was my last coherent thought before the world faded to black.

Chapter Five

Logan

The firecracker asleep by my side looked so angelic, the little snores from her cupid's bow of a mouth endearing her to me all the more. She had to be worn out. *Five times last night, a new record.*

I wondered what her real name was…and how in hell had she known mine? That had to be some lucky guess…unless it was all a ruse. No, she didn't come off that way. She came off as an honest soul, fueled by an intense interest in life. I admired that. Nothing worse than a jaded person. And the best part? Her passion and responses to my attentions were off-the-charts hot. This one I wanted to experience again and again. Until that fire burned out, though I couldn't imagine that happening anytime soon.

I slipped out of bed and headed for the shower, which was when it hit me that I had an interview with the librarian lady in an hour. I groaned aloud as I stepped into the running water and began washing the heady scent of our recent lovemaking from my body. And here I was wanting to take my angel out to breakfast before heading back to the room for a Sunday matinee that could last until Monday morning, if she was up to it. I was more than capable—just thinking about her was making me hard all over again.

Towel wrapped around my waist, I strode back into the bedroom only to find her dressing and looking cute with her long hair in complete disarray, her cheeks flushed with color.

"Morning, angel." I crossed the room in a couple of strides, hoping to entice her back to bed.

"Oh, morning. Sorry, I have to get going. I have something pressing I must do today."

I bent my head and kissed the velvet-smooth skin of her neck, brushing her hair aside to gain better access. "Are you certain it can't wait?"

"Dead certain. My job depends on it."

She seemed distracted and I frowned. Where was the passionate woman I had met and enjoyed all night? Well, if her job depended on it, it was excusable, of course.

"Too bad. I had hoped to take you to breakfast. Say, it would be nice to exchange real names now. Not like we don't know each other well enough," I hinted.

"No, I'm good." She turned her back and pointed at her zipper. "If you don't mind?"

Disappointed and horny, I pulled up the zip and turned her around so that we faced each other. I gave her a lingering kiss, her lips burning against mine. Her pliable body increased the pressure in my groin. She wanted to stay. I'd bet on it. Her scent of arousal drove me crazy, my wolf even pushing to appear. That had to be stopped from happening, of course, but it took some doing on my part. Strange, that hadn't happened before. Maybe the reason was that I needed to make time for him. It couldn't be because of the gorgeous female I had made love to all night long, could it? I needed to call Lachlan if that were the case, to get his take on this.

"I'm Logan, by the way. You must be psychic, guessing my real name like that."

Her beautiful blue eyes widened. "Really? That is something. Now, I gotta go."

"Quid pro quo, angel."

She began to back away, looking a bit panicked. "Look, I'm sorry, okay? I'm just so late and I need to shower before my meeting. I smell like you."

"Yes, you do." I grinned widely, almost enjoying her discomfort…knowing she was totally aroused. She too was suffering, making her need to leave me easier to take. She was doomed to find any other male unable to take care of her like I could.

I watched her leave, envisioning many nights of pleasure to come.

The phone rang and I answered it, still distracted by blue eyes. Damn. I forgot to get her number. Well, she'd be back knocking at my door before nightfall.

"Logan here."

"It's Madelyn Smith. I just sent the twins your way. You need to have a talk with them, remind them their conduct is not acceptable. Naked in the fountain! What is this—the Roaring Twenties? This is a respectable casino, Mr. Creig."

"Of course. Send them to my suite. I'll take care of it before my appointment with the professor from the university."

I frowned, annoyed that my off-the-cuff moment in the pub back home was biting me in the ass in Vegas. Now I most likely had to send the pair home. Unless I could see a huge difference in their attitude this morning, ready to make amends, they were headed back to the Highlands on the next commercial airliner.

A loud knocking on the door and I strode across the room, annoyed as hell. A night to remember followed by this shit.

Three women stood in my doorway. Holy shit. My angel was propping up one of the twins, her expression beyond exasperated. The twins were almost naked, wearing only transparent lingerie that would be better suited to a Victoria's Secret catalog, and the rank odor of alcohol slammed into my olfactory nerves.

She gave me a steely-eyed look that made my stomach plummet. "Apparently these two belong to you?" Her frigid tone further suggested just how far she was from my passionate partner of the night before.

"Yes, unfortunately. Thank you for assisting them."

"Look, it's Loki-Logan, our favorite trickster," one twin said with a slight slur, grabbing for my arm while attempting to kiss me. I couldn't say which one it was that I peeled off me and assisted to the sofa. They looked too alike and I was too angry to differentiate. I didn't want what my angel and I had experienced last night to end on this sour note.

"I apologize for this. Please, just go to your meeting and I'll take care of it. They've had a little too much to drink."

She raised an eyebrow at me and brushed past me, helping the other twin join her sister. Then she stormed out, slamming the door.

"I don't think she liked us." One twin giggled. "Especially when we told her how much we owe you. You know, choosing us to accompany you to Vegas for some fun. Two is better than one in making a Loki-Logan-Love sandwich."

The pair erupted into peals of laughter. It was all I could do not to strangle them on the spot. What would my angel think of this? I needed to explain the situation. Then I remembered I didn't even have her phone number.

I raked my hands through my hair. Maybe it was time to quit thinking all women were my personal playground. The woman from last night was so far above any female I had met in so long that it was like she was from another planet.

"You two are headed home on the next plane." I made my displeasure clear with crossed arms and a steely-eyed look.

"*Phttt.* You're no fun!"

The other stuck her tongue at me. *Christ on a cracker.* This pair would be the death of me. "You stay here and sleep this off. Do not move from this room. I have an interview in my office to take care of. Then I'll be back. Are we clear?"

"Yes, Captain Loki-Logan." They said the words in chorus then saluted before falling against each other in a giggle fit.

I just shook my head, disgusted with myself for being an idiot and bringing them along. Well, they'd be headed home today, no questions asked. I just hoped I could find my angel and explain the circumstances. Not that the actual facts of the case sounded all that good in hindsight. I left the suite and headed for the elevator, needing to check how much damage this pair had caused before the interview. *Good thing the Creig clan has extra-deep pockets.*

Then I'd have a detective track down my angel.

Chapter Six

Justine

I couldn't believe it. The guy I thought was so perfect last night was a ladies' man, a Casanova, a womanizer to the nth degree. The kind of man I would never, ever, even if he were the last man on Earth, be involved with. Not that I was. It had just been one glorious night. A meeting of two needy people for one extremely fabulous night of amazing sex. But still. I sure couldn't pick them any better than my mom. Disgusted with myself, I slammed my front door, stomped through the house and stepped into the shower. I had exactly thirty-seven minutes to clean up and be back at the casino for my meeting with the movie director. I groaned. Like that was going to be any fun.

As I stood in the stream of water, my mind slipped back to the night before and my body came alive, feeling his hands on me, touching me in all the right ways. That tongue of his should come with a warning sign—*Beware of Too Many Orgasms.*

Whoa, I had another climax just thinking of it. I jumped out and dried off, then ran around pulling together an outfit that screamed I'm-a-damn-professional-and-don't-you-forget-it.

I looked around frantically for my cell phone and remembered that bridezilla still had it. *Shoot.* I could only imagine the angry people I had literally abandoned last night. *Well, nothing for it now.* I had to get back to the casino and get that damn interview over with, then make my round of apologies. This day was just getting better and better. What was going to happen now? Maybe an earthquake to add to the misery?

A loud pounding on the front door settled it. Someone was already on the case, looking to bust my lady balls.

I gathered up my briefcase to haul along to the meeting and slipped my laptop into it to make notes, just in case the director had exact specifications for what he wanted to achieve. My luck, he'd be a pie-in-the-sky guy and just share his vision minus the details, like that was going to be useful. I was a detail person first and foremost.

I opened the front door to be confronted by Marnie. *Could be worse.*

"Thank goodness you're home."

Guilt stabbed me at the concern on my friend's face. I should have let her know what was going on last night, but it'd all began in such a whirlwind, I still wasn't exactly sure what had occurred myself. *Other than I lost my damn mind.*

"Sorry, girlfriend. Can we walk and talk? I'm late for a meeting that'll have the dean biting off my head if I miss it."

Marnie turned and joined me in walking to the curb to my vehicle, where I fumbled for my keys and unlocked the door. "What happened last night?" she asked, her arms crossed over her chest. "Jane and Ellen are about to disown you. You disappeared and had everyone worried."

"I know. But Jane had my phone." *Lame, but true.*

"Last I heard you were looking for your earring. You're looking awfully good for a gal who drank what we did last night. What's up? You hook up with someone on the way to the bathroom?" she asked with a laugh, like that was an impossibility.

I remained silent.

"What? No way! You did, right? Hell, girlfriend, I didn't know you had it in you."

"Not my finest moment, okay? But I gotta run now. Please, tell me you rescued our phones?"

"Right. One of the reasons I'm here." Marnie handed me my lifeline.

"Thank you." I gave her an extra-long hug. "And thanks for coming by. I'm sorry I worried you. I'll call you right after the interview, okay?"

"You'd better. Right, I'm out of here. Just glad you're okay. Now go. Channel your inner captain with that director. You got this."

Feeling like a first-class heel, I managed a small smile for my friend's boating reference and climbed into my SUV. A quick wave and I hit the road. Time was getting away from me and I hated being late. I pressed my foot flat to the floorboards, gunning the vehicle.

With one minute to spare, I raced down the hallway of the casino after getting directions to the film director's office from the front desk. I stopped at the door, took a deep breath in an effort to lower my heart rate then went inside, hoping I looked more in control than I felt.

Like everything in the Glitter Palace, the décor was scrumptious in the spacious reception area — chairs covered in soft, inviting cream-colored leather, seascapes that looked into another world on the walls and a huge tile and chrome desk that was definitely upscale, with its high-tech gadgetry. But the area was abandoned. Well, it was Sunday. Was I supposed to just walk into the office marked *Director*?

Well, what else was there to do? There wasn't a time clock I could punch and let it be known I had not arrived late. Hmm, well maybe I could just sit quietly, not be noticed, then leave if no one appeared, so that at least I could say my obligations had been met? Then I'd be off the hook, right? Okay, I'd give it ten minutes.

I sat and pulled out my cell phone, then groaned at the multitude of messages, most marked *urgent*. Yup, Jane had gone ballistic while Ellen was threatening me with legal action. I answered as best I could, then shut off my phone. Maybe there was an upside to all this? No more invites to be a bridesmaid? All my experiences to date had been less than stellar.

I tapped my toes. One more minute and I could leave with impunity. My mind drifted back to the night's shenanigans, my body overheating at the memory. I took a deep, shuddering breath. I had to get that man right out of my mind!

Okay. I was so out of here. I stood up to leave and heard a door open.

"Is my ten o'clock here yet?"

That voice. It sounded familiar. My blood turned to fire as a familiar face and body suddenly stood in the now too-small reception area.

"You!" The word slipped out before I could hold it back.

We locked eyes. The force of his charisma hit me like a blast of heat escaping the world's hottest furnace. *Oh. My. Lord.*

"What are you doing here?" I blurted, like my mind and common sense had lost touch.

"This is my office. You must know that if you've tracked me down?" He smiled a bit too smugly.

"Tracked you down! No way. I'm here to see the director of the movie. I have an appointment." I shook my head so hard I about gave myself a concussion.

Realization hit him between the eyes. "You're Professor Justine Bell from the university?"

"Uh, yeah. But who are you?"

"Logan Creig, the director of the movie."

Stunned, I couldn't speak. How in the nine hells of creation had this happened? Karma had just bitten me in the ass. The one time I let myself go astray and this shit happened?

"Well, this is interesting," he said, a grin enveloping his gorgeous mug.

I swallowed. Logan Creig. A first name I loved that would now live in infamy. How could I have made such a huge mistake? I was normally such a reserved, careful person. I didn't take chances. And yet here I was, in the biggest mess of my life. This just couldn't be happening.

"How about we talk in my office?"

He turned to lead the way and without thinking, I dutifully followed. How was I going to get out of this? Working with the guy I was insanely attracted to spelled trouble with the biggest T in creation. And he had other women on a string, judging by the two prancing into his hotel room earlier. My judgment was in the dungeon. No one, as long as I lived, could know about this insanity on my part.

I sat stiffly across from my nemesis, crossing my legs and making sure my thighs were decently covered by the hem of my skirt. I'd chosen a power suit and a high-necked blouse that now threatened to strangle me. I eased one finger under the collar to loosen the fabric. Why was the room so darn warm all of a sudden?

I chanced a glance at Logan and was met with a smoldering look. Time to grow some lady balls.

"You teach at the university and have a strong background in Egyptian antiquities. I have a shipment arriving today that will require assessment. I need an inventory list completed as soon as possible. Is that a problem for you, Justine?"

The informal use of my name grated and I clenched my teeth together as I shook my head.

"No, it's not a problem?"

"No, it's not a problem because this isn't going to work," I said, gripping my hands together in my lap so hard my fingernails bit into my palms.

"Why not? Not like we aren't already acquainted in a most intimate way." He smiled, his eyes suddenly appearing greener and more mesmerizing.

I broke the look first. *I need to get the hell out of here.* "It's not going to work because it's not professional." It sounded lame even to me.

"What? Not professional to have a relationship with the director?"

"We don't have a relationship! We had a one-night stand."

"I would so enjoy it becoming more than that. Maybe even an every-night stand."

"You're not listening to me! We can't be an item. I don't want to be a cliché. Director's casting couch and all that." The thought of our insanely passionate night together, awesome as it had been, being discussed by others made my skin crawl.

"It doesn't have to be like that."

"Right. And how about those two women earlier? Looks like the casting couch is a ticking time bomb."

"I sent them packing back to Scotland. You won't be bothered by them again."

That was something, anyway. Sitting up straighter, I racked my brain for a way out of this nightmare. If only I wasn't so damn attracted to Logan, then maybe I could do this thing. Then again, maybe my job wouldn't bring us into daily contact? I was working on antiquities, not as an actress in his film. *No need to be brushing elbows every two minutes.*

"Tell me again how you see this thing unfolding?"

"Between you and me? Well, let me see, I think I would enjoy slowly undoing that librarian blouse and letting down that gorgeous hair of yours. Then running my fingers through the silky strands while I kiss the soft skin of your slender neck. A string of hot kisses all the way down to your perfect breasts, where I'd suck on the nipples until you cried aloud your need, begging me to take you. And I would, but not until I'd pushed your beautiful thighs apart and applied my tongue in long, velvety strokes to your throbbing clit. Then I would suck—"

"Stop right there!" Horrified and more turned on than I would have ever imagined possible, I stood, knocking over my chair. The throbbing between my legs was insane. "No way can I work for you!"

I raced from the room, slamming the door. I had to get out of there or I would have jumped him right then and there. Fucked him on his desk and not worried for a second if anyone came in. Turned on didn't begin to cover it. I was out of my damn mind with lust and passion.

"Justine! Come back."

I ignored Logan and rushed from the office. If I didn't get away now I was doomed.

Chapter Seven

Logan

Well, we'd see about that. My wolf begged to be released to chase her and I had to stamp down on the sensation, hard. What was that? I pulled out my phone and made a call to the very useful dean at the university. It wouldn't be appropriate to run through the casino following her. I didn't need or want that kind of attention. But Justine would be back in my bed and keeping me warm before nightfall. The scent of her arousal had nearly done me in.

I shouldn't have taunted her like that, but she didn't even know about this pull between us, that she'd never escape it until it burned out. If it ever did. Well, I would have to think for the both of us for now. She desperately required me to take care of her needs or she wouldn't be able to function. And I was just the wolf to do it. But a quick call to my brother wouldn't go amiss. *Anything to keep my mind busy.*

I brought up Lachlan's number, punched it in and waited for him to answer.

"Hey, bro. How's the movie business treating you?" Lachlan's voice was clear as a bell, like he was right next to me at the dinner table back home.

"Good. How's things on your end?" I stalled, not certain how to ask what I wanted to know.

"Fine. You were just home. What's up? You meet someone?" His voice had a smile in it. But how in the hell did he know that?

"Well, just one fabulous woman that's driving my wolf to distraction," I deadpanned.

"Hmm. And you just met?" Lachlan gave a chuckle. "Never thought I'd see the day."

"What? It was just one night of passion. Sure, it was the best night imaginable. But that doesn't mean—"

"You want to keep that wolf under control, you'd best let him have his time, bro. Give him a run in the desert. Not like Cristaldo doesn't have the land for it."

"Yeah, point taken." The advice was welcome and easy enough to follow.

"Keep me informed. I've been there. Trust me, you're going to need all the help you can get."

I hung up on another chuckle. *Thanks a lot.*

I cleared up some paperwork while I waited for the vastly more interesting reappearance of the errant antiquities expert. I vowed to control myself when she reappeared. And just where in the hell was she? Her boss should have had her ass back here by now. And what a beautiful ass it was.

A tentative knock on my door made me smile. I ran a hand through my hair, then got up to answer the call. It had to be my angel by the delicious scent of roses and honey wafting under the door.

We locked eyes with each other. Hers were wide with emotion, and I'm certain mine were glinting with my inner predator. He was certainly pushing inside me. I would have to step up my game, make time for him in the desert.

"You're back." It was not a question.

She swallowed and the graceful slim column of her neck moved as her chin rose. "Yes, I am."

I nodded. "Good."

"What do you need me to do first?"

Fuck me. Then fuck me again. Instead, I said, "Check out this list." I retrieved it from my desk, handing it to her.

"The Egyptian antiquities," she said.

She took it from me, our fingers brushing in the process. I watched her pupils dilate. She was so near the edge. It would take so little to have her under my control. This was going to be too much damn fun. I wished I had been party to what her boss had said. Was I feeling even a bit guilty to have pulled the dean into it? Made sure she was sent back to me? No, not one iota. That was not the way of the wolf. *We take what's ours.* Justine was now under my protection. I would be the one to make sure she was always all right. Whatever it took, I would be there for her.

"I'll go and check on things now. Do you have a key for the storage room or prop room or whatever it's called that houses the artifacts?"

I pulled the access card from my desk and handed it over. "Prop room. Main floor. I appreciate your doing this."

"Like I had a choice in the matter!" The words spilled out, obviously before she could think. She pinkened. I could only imagine how warm her beautiful body was right now, all flushed and flustered.

She must have known what I was thinking, because she turned away, taking the key and list with her. I smiled. "I'll check on you in a couple of hours. Unless you'd like to go for an early lunch?"

"Not hungry."

Wrong, angel, you're starving and it's not going to let up. You just don't know that yet.

I turned back to my paperwork, my mind in a better place to focus now that she was under my roof. I'd give her a little time to work her mind around things—it seemed the gentlemanly thing to do. *Like I'm a gentleman.* I snorted at the idea. Hmm. I wondered if I could talk her into taking a small role in the movie? It would be easy enough to add a few lines from the antiquities expert that would help drive the plot.

Picking up my cell, I pulled up the head writer's number and made the call. "I need to see you in my office," I said over the phone.

"Be right there."

Five minutes later, Valerie knocked on my open office door to alert me to her presence.

"Thanks for coming on such short notice," I said.

Valerie favored me with a rueful smile. Her dark mass of hair was pulled into a messy, stylish bun and her face devoid of makeup as usual. She was a good-looking woman, but her brain was even prettier, having been a great help so far in helping create my vision. "I expected more calls in the middle of the night so I'm good. The last director always seemed to have his best ideas for a rewrite at three a.m. Without fail. At least yours arrive at a decent hour."

"Shall we get down to it?" I laid out what I wanted.

"Yeah, it's actually an excellent idea. Adds more credibility to the script as well. Got any idea of who should play the expert, or do you want me to check with casting?" Valerie asked.

"I do. The actual expert."

I pulled up my screensaver to show Valerie a photo of my angel.

"She might be too good-looking to be taken seriously."

"But moviegoers love beautiful characters and she's an actual antiquities expert in real life, hired by me. That can be listed in the credits. Right now, she's on site and working with movie props for our big finale."

"Okay then. I'll have a contract drawn up. I should check in with her to get all her details."

I nodded. "Go ahead. She's in the prop room."

Valerie got to her feet, tucked her laptop snugly back in its case and left to take care of things.

I'd give Valerie enough time to pull off getting the contract signed, then I'd head in and take a happy angel to brunch. What woman didn't want to see herself on the big screen? Not to mention it would increase our working time together. And with all the tension and sexuality simmering so effortlessly between us, it would add another source of excitement to the film. *Win-win.*

The only thing better would be if I was the leading man in the movie and she was my love interest. Now *that* onscreen chemistry would guarantee that viewers were glued to the screen. Especially if it was an R rated product like the *Fifty Shades* franchise. We'd turn that audience on and make their world so exciting that everyone would get lucky after the show ended.

"No fucking way!"

I looked up from my computer screen, annoyed by the interruption. In my mind my angel and I were enjoying the fruits of having another successful movie in the can. *Celebrating in bed, of course.*

I pursed my lips, taking in the tantalizing view of breasts heaving. Why was Justine spitting mad and standing in my office? Had Valerie done something to set her off? I couldn't imagine that happening. My head writer had such a level head on her shoulders.

"You'll need to explain that better," I advised.

"I'm not going to act in a movie. Are we clear?"

Confused, I sat back in my chair. "Why on earth not?"

"Because I'm not an actress."

"Good. We want authenticity."

She huffed. "Then because I don't want to, okay?"

"But you're *perfect* for the part. And just think of the publicity for the university."

Her expression shifted, less sure now. She knew I had her. "Tell me you're not going to call over to where I work again and make me look bad?"

"Not if I don't have to. Come on. It's something you should be pleased about. Plus, big bonus, we get to work even more closely together." I would see to it she was sneaked into enough scenes that she'd be at my beck and call the entire time. *Might as well throw in the towel right now, Professor. The big bad wolf* always *wins.*

"*That* is not a bonus."

She was so beautiful when she was angry. Almost as beautiful as when she was pliant in my hands. The fates had been kind to me, bringing this angel into my life. I should have visited Vegas years ago.

"I disagree."

She stared me down, but she was the first to look away.

"Would you care for brunch now?"

She rolled her eyes like a teenager. "You never give up, do you?"

"Never. It's written in my DNA. All the Creigs are known for that characteristic. You should meet our matriarch, The Creig. She's the epitome of stubborn. But she gets it done and keeps a firm hand on the reins."

"Female. I like that. I'll get back to work then."

"And sign that contract. Then we can celebrate."

She flipped me the bird so unexpectedly that I laughed aloud as she stormed out of my office. What a naughty angel!

Chapter Eight

Justine

I stormed out of Logan's office. *Of all the nerve!* Logan assuming I'd be enticed by such an enterprise — well, he didn't know me at all. Okay, honestly, maybe a tiny, little piece of me was flattered. But I was bigger than that. I'd never coast on my looks or use them to manipulate my way in the system. I wanted to be taken seriously more than anything. *Valued for my brain.*

With my mind so tied up that I ignored my surroundings, I just about bumped into Valerie in the reception area, the woman who had created the new problem for me. Maybe that wasn't quite fair — she was just the messenger after all.

"Are we good?" Valerie asked, the contract I was supposed to sign clutched in her hands.

"Yeah, sure, why not." I grabbed the pen she offered, set the contract on the desk and scribbled my name beside the X.

"You don't sound very excited about the opportunity," she said. "Why did you change your mind?"

I had flatly refused to sign at first. "Blackmail."

Her eyebrows rose over intense emerald-green eyes. I'd never seen so many green-colored eyes in my life since Logan came to town. Weren't they the rarest of irises? Rarer even than blue. Yes, two percent came to mind. Ah, there was one color found even less in the human population, gray.

Of course, that made me think of the movie *Fifty Shades of Grey* and that was no help. I could just imagine Logan being in his element if I was to become a submissive. Would that be such a bad thing? He was so damn alpha to my feminine mystique. Hours and hours spent playacting in bed was beyond enticing. Thoughts of allowing that talented master to bring out all my lustful fantasies tugged at my imagination and other parts, bringing me up short. *Damn it, Justine, keep your mind on business.*

"I seriously doubt you have to do this if you don't want to, right?"

I didn't want the woman to feel bad about it. It wasn't her fault that Logan and I had got off to such a rocky beginning. Maybe that was the wrong word. Make that explosive beginning, like two stars colliding in the night sky. But I had to be careful or I would burn up. Every time I thought of him, my body craved his touch. And no, that wasn't a good thing when I'd worked so damn hard to be accepted as a professional.

I did not have time for a whirlwind romance, or whatever this thing was. I was choosing to stay single and keep my eye on the prize and had zero time for anything else. How often had I discussed this with my girlfriends? A lot and with good reason.

"No. I just had reservations. But that's all cleared up now."

"Good." The woman looked relieved. "Then things are settled. I'll file this contract and have you sent a permanent one after all the parties sign."

"Thank you."

I exited the room and headed back to props, forcing my mind back to what I was there for. I had to admit, I was enjoying that part of the job immensely. Such interesting finds had made their way to Vegas from Egypt. All fabulous fakes, of course, but still, one never knew if a real McCoy might have been tucked in by accident. Like a child at Christmas, I thrilled to be unwrapping the gifts. But I certainly wouldn't be sharing that with Logan any time soon.

I closed the door to the slightly musty prop room with its rows of shelving and boxes of wooden crates just waiting to be cataloged. It was a special room, kept at the proper humidity and with low lighting, adding to the thrill of the search.

I had unloaded the smaller crates before the contract fiasco, having found great works of art that had been recreated by a brilliant professional. Amulets made of the pure gold so plentiful in the Nile Valley and that were worth a fortune if real were lined up on a shelf, all cataloged and ready for insertion in the specially designed boxes for display in the movie. The golden death mask of Tut looked so authentic I wasn't convinced it was a fake, certain that at the very least it had been overlaid with gold leaf and authentic jewels. I had left the largest box for last. What mysteries did it hold?

Grabbing the prybar, I turned my attention to it, slipping the iron rod under the lid and popping up the nails that held it fastened to the base. The squawks of steel and wood separating filled the space, making my ears ring. Ignoring the sensation, I was totally focused on what was inside, heart beating like a wild drum.

Finally, after a lot of loud shrieks, I was able to pull the lid aside and take a look at the contents. Peering into the crate, I discovered the large coffin—more officially recognized as a sarcophagus—covered in layers of dingy cotton batting. *Odd choice.* All the others had used modern bubble wrap.

I'd never be able to get all the wrapping off without totally dismantling the box. Dismayed, I decided to cut away what I could and at least get a peek at the artifact. My stomach grumbled just as I grabbed a pair of shears to attack the covering.

"Soon, okay. I just want a glimpse," I said.

The ancient batting filled the air with spores and dust as I cut into it, making me sneeze relentlessly, my eyes streaming tears. The bubble wrap was much nicer. But I persisted and uncovered a small section. Running my hands over the dirt-encrusted lid, I detected engravings. *Nice.* My heart rate speeded up. This wasn't at all what I'd expected. The rest of the entries were made to look authentic, but they weren't filthy like this odd one was. What was it doing here? Desperate to get a closer look, I grabbed up the crowbar again and set to work.

In no time I was sweaty and covered in a film of grime. But oh boy, I was in my element. Hieroglyphics were so intriguing when they were engraved on objects to tell an ancient story. I couldn't wait to find out what the engravings revealed. It was obvious the box hadn't been opened in a very long time. Centuries, maybe, even not since the days of the pharaohs. What was it doing with the rest of the stuff? It could be a hoax. But who would play such an elaborate one?

My stomach grumbled again and I sighed. Starving didn't even cover it. Last night had expended a great number of calories. I shoved a strand of hair wearily back with my hand and a wave of dizziness and a shower of sparks swept across my vision.

I would have to finish this job later. I needed to wash up and eat before I succumbed to exhaustion. What time was it anyway? I was on my hands and knees now, struggling with the damn box.

The door opened, letting in the light. Surrounded by a huge halo, Logan's figure appeared even larger, like a feudal lord descending from another realm. I shook my head. I must have been hallucinating from lack of food. But now that he was there, other needs stirred. Why was I so drawn to a man I had just met, all the amazing sex aside? It defied explanation.

"You need to eat, my angel."

"My name is Justine. And yes, I do." I got to my feet but swayed from the suddenness of the movement.

He was immediately at my side, offering support. "Are you all right?"

I shrugged off his hand. "I'm fine."

"This is unacceptable. You should never go hungry. Come. I'll feed you."

"What century is this anyway?" I made light of his concern. "I can feed myself, you know. But first I need to wash up. I'm covered in dust."

"There's a bathroom right outside."

I hurried away, leaving him standing there. Pushing open the door marked *Ladies*, I caught a glimpse of myself in the mirror and groaned. I needed a shower, but the sink would have to do.

I cupped my hands and splashed cold water onto my face. Refreshed, I dried off and smoothed down my hair. Hurrying back into the hallway, I found Logan waiting and texting on his phone.

"Ready?" he asked, his eyes lighting up at my reappearance.

"Best I can manage."

"You look beautiful. Well, except for this." He reached up and tugged something from the back of my hair, giving me a sense of déjà vu. He quickly disposed of it in the nearest refuse container.

"Not an earring this time?" I quipped.

"No, a spider." Logan frowned, not responding to my joke.

"*Oh my God!* Did you get it?" I was deathly afraid of spiders and began to shake and awkwardly dance about, making sure it had gone away. *Arachnophobia's a pain in the ass.* But not only were spiders creepy, they could be dangerous.

"Yes, it's gone."

"What kind was it?" I shuddered, certain that there had to be something else crawling on me. I knew I'd never shake the feeling until I showered and inspected every inch of my body.

"A small black widow."

That settled it. "I have to shower."

"Of course."

He led the way while I strode purposely at his side, trying not to grimace and shiver with every step. We stepped into the elevator and though it only took a few seconds to reopen at Logan's floor, it took far too long in my opinion.

"Through there. I'll find you something to wear."

"Thanks." I was grateful for his not overreacting to my need to wash off where some people would roll their eyes and be terribly condescending. I saw nothing of that in his expression or attitude, only concern.

I yanked off my sweaty clothing, dumping it on the floor before climbing into the huge glass and chrome stall with the lovely rain shower effect. Soaping and scrubbing, I barely noticed how hungry I was, so intent on becoming squeaky clean. No red marks appeared on my skin though I inspected it thoroughly, so I must have gotten off lightly. Black widow bites, though bad, didn't usually kill their victim, but could make one quite ill or discomforted at the least.

I heard the door opening and braced myself for Logan's possible reappearance. I wouldn't put it past him to join me, but strangely enough, the door closed, leaving me alone. Suddenly feeling bereft, I shut off the water and wrapped myself in a huge fluffy white bath sheet. My thoughts jumbled, I quickly dried off and pulled my hair back from my face with a wide-toothed comb.

Looking around, I spied articles of clothing hanging on the hook behind the door. Logan must have left them for me, because they hadn't been there earlier. *Hmm.* A lovely midi dress in blue silk with the price tag still attached. Even fresh underwear. And he'd judged my size quite accurately. Fancy for a Sunday brunch, but in keeping with what he wore — expensive tailored suits from some big-name company, I was dead certain. Clothes weren't that important to me, but I had to admit, it felt nice to have the silky fabric slither down my body and hug all my curves in the most flattering of ways. The guy had great taste.

I opened my bag and pulled out a small makeup case. No way was I going to reappear looking anything but professional after that panic attack. I shook my head. *What must he think of me?* But, in my defense, it wasn't a harmless daddy long legs but a deadly black widow.

I dried my hair with the blow dryer I found in one of the drawers and brushed it smooth with a central part. With the mascara I'd applied darkening my eyelashes, pale powder hiding the shine on my nose and a swipe of rose-pink glistening on my lips, I looked about ready for anything.

When I exited the bathroom, I read the truth of it in Logan's eyes as he gave a low wolf whistle. "The most beautiful angel of all time. You're going to be a knockout in the movie. I predict you'll show up for a cameo in every scene."

I blushed in spite of my annoyance at being manipulated. I mean, was there a woman alive who didn't like to be thought of as beautiful? "I can't manage my workload if you increase it. I have students to teach during the mornings, so all I can manage is the afternoons and most evenings. I can get someone to help with the marking, but please, don't add me to every scene."

"I'll talk to the dean again. I'm certain he'll release you for the five weeks of filming in Vegas. The press for the university will be incredible, with one of their professors on the big screen."

I shook my head. "I love my job teaching young minds, so I'd rather you didn't do that. Just keep my appearances to a minimum and all will be fine."

He pursed his lips, a speculative look narrowing his eyes. "No can do, angel. I need you in my film *and* I need your expertise. Is it my fault you're perfect for the job?"

Stymied for the moment, I changed the subject to safer ground. "The mask of Tut. Who did the facsimile? It's marvelously done. It feels like solid gold and the garnets shine with authenticity. Hard to believe it's a fake."

He smiled, the action lighting up his entire face. I swallowed. Yup, way too good-looking. *And don't forget, he's a ladies' man, just like your father. Right!* I looked away, pretending to smooth my skirt.

"That copy is made of the same substances and materials as the original."

"Are you saying it's solid gold, not covered in gold foil?" My blood heated up, imagining the cost of such a thing.

"I wanted the display of Egyptian antiquities stolen in the heist to be as authentic as possible. I have the money, so why not make perfect copies of the mask and the other items that will be featured in the casino display?"

He shrugged like that was just the cost of doing business, while my mouth hung open. Good thing another spider didn't happen by.

"The mask is eleven kilograms of gold. Gold is going for around fifty-seven thousand, four hundred dollars a kilogram. That's well over half a million dollars for the gold alone in that one item! Aren't you worried about someone stealing it?"

"The room is kept locked. But don't lose the key card," he joked.

"It's not a joking matter! Exactly how rich are you? What if something happens? I don't want to be blamed."

He came right up to me, putting his arms around me as if to shelter me from the storms of life. "Nobody will ever harm you *ever* again. You have my word on it. My pledge to you is to keep you safe from harm. And on that note, you need to eat before anything else. You need your strength for what lies ahead."

The gleam in his eyes told the story. He was expecting me to jump into bed with him again. *No way.* I was *not* going to let that happen. Now that he was technically my immediate boss, we had to keep our distance. It would be insanity to do otherwise. The reasons not to be with Logan were growing by the hour.

But oh, the temptation...

Even starving as I was for sustenance, looking at that man, strong, bold and handsome, breathing in his heady manly fragrance, caused a thrumming in my blood as if fired by ancient sources. It took my breath clear away like romance novels had always hinted, my knees getting weaker by the second. The urge to lie down on a bed—or any flat surface for that matter, as long as it was with Logan... Who needed food when a warrior stood by their side, promising the best sex ever?

I knew the split second his blood caught fire to match my own. His eyes flashed such an intense green I swore I became dazzled, able to see only him. Everything else around him vanished. Softened. While he became all. *Focus, Justine. Set the parameters of whatever this thing is before one of us gets hurt.* And that would probably be me, if history repeated itself.

"No offense, but I'm not looking for anything more than sex. Just so you know." The sex was off the charts, but I was keeping my heart protected at all costs. *I can do that, right?*

For a moment he seemed nonplussed, almost a little hurt, like I had caught him off guard. But that couldn't be right, because I knew he was a ladies' man. The twins more than proved it. All I had to do was keep my heart on lockdown and I could enjoy our bodies to the max.

"If that's what you want, angel. I just want to be with you, whatever it takes. Live this moment to its fullest."

"We can agree on that."

Then he bent his head and kissed me, stopping any more words from forming in my overheated brain. I shamelessly slipped my tongue into his mouth, then sucked on his when he responded. A moan escaped one of us. Nothing in my life could have prepared me for this obsessive desire, overwhelming lust and acute need to be with a man.

He crushed me to his chest, and the long length of his body pressed intimately against mine, all solid muscle to my soft curves. A glorious fit. Unbelievable. Every square inch of me heated, tingling with anticipation. I had a better chance of being hit by lightning than being able to move away from the feast that this highlander promised and delivered.

"Oh, my angel. What you do to me," he whispered in a tone that was filled with reverence and smoldering excitement. He ran a finger down my cheek to slip across my lips, making my lower body thrum with an overpowering need.

My clothes were stifling me and I whispered back, taking a chance that he would see this for what it was and join in the game. If I could do that, then I could keep the two parts of my life separate. "Please, sir, I need to feel your naked flesh on mine."

In a twinkling of an eye, my dress slipped off my shoulders and pooled on the floor. My underwear followed, before Logan removed all of his clothes, standing before me all tan flesh and ripped, his six-pack so pronounced it appeared carved from steel.

I took a second to run my hands over his perfect body, appreciating the moment in time that seemed to hover so blissfully before us. Endless hours of pure fucking. No commitments. He gave me a crooked grin, so endearing that my heart squeezed, before pulling me into his arms again. My breasts pressed against him, swelling from the delicious contact, nipples begging for attention.

He picked me up and laid me down on the bed, leaving some distance between us as he admired my body.

I wanted to show him how turned on being with him made me, slipping my hands down to my breasts, enjoying the weight and fullness. I ran my fingers around the tips, the nipples hardening instantly, then tugged on the sensitive nubs, making myself moan, making him moan. Our eyes locked, the urge to be together, to mate, undeniable. It thrummed between us, alive, while the world dropped away.

The urgent need for release grew, made me spread my legs, exposing myself. I closed my eyes and thought of his hands on my breasts. His lips on my nipples. His cock hard and pushing against my slick folds. I wanted to feel that loss of control, allow myself to be free of every restraint.

Then he was doing exactly as I imagined. His strong hands touching all of me, his eyes still locked on mine as he caressed my body. An alpha lover, he gave full attention to exactly what I craved. Sharing everything, holding nothing back.

He entered me as soon as he'd pulled on a condom, piercing my body with his hugeness. Stretching me, filling me. Making me do his bidding.

I bucked against him, my thighs clutching him for greater depth. He reached down between us, gaining access to my clit. It throbbed, and he tugged at it, the swollen nub pulsating with pleasure. So pleasurable I would turn myself inside out for it to continue. I had no choice, no say—it was as essential to my being as the tide ebbing and flowing around the world on any given day.

"Take me. Harder." My voice and body were swept along as he rolled me over onto my stomach, taking me from behind. Without preamble, he thrust in and out in a rapid tempo, pistoning into my body. I was close. *So close.* My body wanted to drop over the precipice, to release itself from the throes of a primal need.

His hands grasped my hips, pulling me up against him, his balls pressed tight against my ass. His body locked into mine. Huge. Hard. Almost unable to take the violation, I moaned as unbelievable pleasure streaked through me…and I was greedy for more.

"That's it, take it all. Let me in, angel. I want all of you. Let me do this—fill you with all of me." His rumbling tone crashed through me. Electrified, I let it happen, let him take control of my body and mind. It was beyond exhilarating, this strange new sensation. It was everything that I never knew I wanted. Never knew existed. Until now.

"I will never hurt you. Let me share all that we are. I will take you beyond anything you could ever imagine possible. Let your body feel the pleasure, stay in the moment."

His words were mesmerizing, not actual words, but something more. An ancient promise that etched across my mind.

"Yes, sir!" The waves crested and my body convulsed with an orgasm that went on and on. Heat and juices mingled in the air, the electrifying aroma of sex.

Then in a happy glow, I lay curled up against him, unable to move from pure exhaustion. I could understand why it was called the little death now. Being on the other side did indeed feel like a rebirth. A new day. A new Justine.

I rolled over finally to find him staring at me, his eyes endless pools of wisdom.

"I'm going to feed you now."

Of course. That was as it should be. This was a night of fantasy, after all.

He got up and left the room, coming back a few seconds later with a white platter rimmed with a wide band of gold. He sat down cross-legged on the bed and I moved to join him. Naked, he set the plate beside us. He chose a grape, then gave me a devilish look, dipping the fruit in the bowl of whipped cream.

"Open," he commanded.

I let my chin drop and he popped the morsel of food into my waiting mouth. The juice of the purple grape exploded on my tongue as I bit into it.

"More," I said, finding it fun, my appetite overtaking me. No one had ever taken the time to feed me before. Such a simple, perfect pleasure. Having Logan in control let the fights for one-upmanship at the university drop completely away, an oasis of pure pleasure in a sea of conflict and turmoil.

He obliged, handfeeding me choice bits of fruit and cheese and pastries. He dabbed at my lips with a napkin in the most gentlemanly manner between bites. It was hard to believe this was the man who'd been ravishing my body a short while ago. Now he was consumed with feeding me.

Finally, I held up a hand in surrender. "Enough. I'm full."

Only then did he partake of foodstuffs himself. I watched him eat, finding even that sexy when Logan was doing it. Who knew everyday occupations could be so intriguing? *Guess it depends on who's involved.*

"Come, we need to shower," he said, setting the empty platter aside.

"Yes, sir, but first I have another idea." I let him know with my eyes what I meant, gaining a full-on grin in return. Sunday brunch would never be the same again.

Chapter Nine

Logan

My angel got to her knees on the floor in front of me in one amazing, graceful motion that fired my blood. She licked her lips and crawled toward me, her naked breasts perfect globes that swayed back and forth with each tiny movement, holding me mesmerized and enthralled.

I leaned forward and bound her long blonde locks in one hand to bring her rosebud mouth that was just begging for it toward me. I would be her sir. Let her playact until she could never imagine leaving me. I saw the need in her to be controlled and it spoke to me on the deepest levels of existence. No harm in that. It would only lock us tighter together, the two of us against the world.

"You want it?" I asked, grabbing my cock with my other hand and guiding it toward her sweet lips. She nodded, staring at my swollen member.

"But first I want to anoint it with cream," she said, her eyes huge in her lovely face.

It took me a moment, but then I knew what she wanted, watching her smear cream on my cock with a finger and lick her lips in anticipation of the treat. I thrust into her mouth, her lips parting as the broad crest pressed against them, her mouth closing over me, silk on steel.

A helpless moan escaped her throat as she sucked eagerly at my cock. She drew on it, her cheeks moving with the effort, giving herself up to the lust flaming through her body.

"That's it. Suck me. Take it all."

She tightened her mouth at the explicit language, reaching one hand down to cup my balls.

My cock filled her mouth, and I pushed toward the back of her throat. Her hands busy with my balls, I reached for a nipple, which jutted out so magnificently from her swollen breasts. I took over the rhythm, thrusting in long strokes past her lips, knowing my expression was savage with lust. I gave her all she wanted and more.

She moaned. I twisted her nipple and she moaned harder, arching her back, giving better access. I reached between her legs and found her soaking wet, her lips extended and wide open, her clit swollen and defiant. I thrust three fingers into her, stretching her. She'd need to be stretched as far as possible to take the extreme girth I was going to allow myself this time.

"You like that." It was not a question but a truth. Her arousal had sharpened, nearly killing me with the instant need to possess her.

She couldn't hold back her moans as she milked the sensitive head of my member with her mouth.

"Ah, angel, that's it. Your mouth — *you* — are amazing."

I chose words to goad her on, and, made hungry for me, she sucked all the harder, drawing me deeper into her throat. But I wanted more. I wanted to sink into that sweet pink pussy of hers. I could not allow myself to brand her mine — not until she understood the full truth of it — but I could make her want only me, the only one who would be able to satisfy her. I longed to stretch her until it was only me who could give her what she needed.

When I was about to come, I pulled out of her mouth. "I want you now. Open for me."

I pulled on a condom and grabbed her hips and held her up, straddling me. I teased her soaking-wet lips and clit with the thick head of my cock, sliding back and forth down her swollen slit. Her breathing became ragged, her skin hotter and more flushed. She was so ready that she was losing control, just like I needed her to be.

She reached down and held herself open, pulling her lips wide apart, exposing her wet pink pussy. Heat pulsed as her desire slicked her entrance, showing her nerve endings burning with a desperate need to be touched, to be rubbed against. Submissive, she had no control, had given it all over to me, her alpha.

When she whimpered, I pushed as far as I could into her in one long, satisfying stroke, and even then, it was not all of me. Her warmth surrounded me, hot and squeezing. *Heaven.*

"So tight," I murmured, losing myself for a moment in the sensation. I was so thick, so huge that I gave her a moment to recover, then thrust myself in time with her movements. She was my dream come true, my perfect woman. The angel of my heart.

"Harder," she ordered.

I needed no other invitation. I buried myself right to the hilt inside her.

She screamed and scratched my back, digging her nails in.

"Are you okay?"

After this, she would never be the same. Her willpower to escape our need to mate would vanish. That was what the legends said. Was it right? Only time would tell. I had a glimpse of understanding that I too wanted to be true what I had always thought a myth.

"Perfect," she said, her voice low and throaty. I reached up and tugged on her nipples, making her squeal and push herself harder against me. Wetness flooded out of her and I wanted to lap it up. She smelled, felt and tasted of heaven. I rubbed myself harder against her clit, savoring the cream it brought, the heat that wrapped my cock.

I had to keep myself in check or I would bite her, mark her as mine so every other male could detect my scent on her. I couldn't do that in good conscience when she didn't understand the ramifications of the act, though every cell in my body screamed to finish it, desperate to make her mine forever. A man or wolf didn't take it lightly to enact the ancient ritual.

"I want to claim you, angel, leave my scent on you that can never be washed away." I declared it anyway, the words uttered in the heat of the moment, my mind focused on a primal event that threatened to overwhelm me the longer we remained connected. My inner wolf howled at me to complete the circle, threatening to break free. I struggled to hold on, wanting to do the right thing, impossible as that felt right now.

"Yes, sir, I want that too." She had no idea what she was asking. Did that matter? Yes. She had to understand first what she was consenting to. I would have to school her first. But she was human. I couldn't tell her anything about us. *It's forbidden.* My mind warred, caught in the impossible situation. But if she were to accidentally become one of us…that would solve all my problems. I could take my time introducing her to the life, help her through the transitions. But would she hate me if I were to go ahead and do the deed without explaining everything fully?

I allowed myself the luxury of barely scraping the surface of her skin with my teeth, teasing her, though in truth it affected me more than her as it was difficult not to finish it. It was like being two entities, one who was civilized and one who was not. I let my body take over then, wanting to release its tension.

As I came, my seed rushing from deep inside my balls until I was weak with it, I realized what was happening. Justine was my fated mate, my Forever Mate. How had I not seen it the first time we made love? But this time, I knew, as the sense of it being a game had dropped away. Problem was, what was I going to do about it now? She wasn't looking for a boyfriend. Hell, she'd even stated in no uncertain terms that this was just sex for her.

The way I had spent my life until now was staring me in the face. I had been unfettered, free to do and be with anyone I wanted. She knew that. Instinctively and concretely with the twin debacle. But now I would have to work to change that low opinion she had of me. Let her see that there was so much more to me than charming the ladies. I had a serious side. One I had come to Vegas to prove in my professional life. I would need to apply that to my personal life going forward.

"We have to shower." Justine's words woke me from my thoughts.

"Yes, we do." I gave her lovely bottom a slap and she gave me wide eyes. I was back in control again, away from the brink of wanting to bite her, but still wanting to test the waters.

"What's that for?" She rubbed her ass cheek with her hand.

"Checking if you like it rough."

She pursed her lips, her expression questioning. "As long as it's not taken too far, sir, I could handle it. If it heightens the sex. Well, if that's possible."

Satisfaction filled me at the compliment. I had more than fulfilled her, obviously. But disappointment hit me that she was still pretending, rather than expressing that this was her real world now, our being together, committing to it.

"Life isn't just sex, angel." My words surprised even me. Up until now, I would never have said such a thing.

"Right now, that's all I want or need, sir," she said with a purr.

Well, we'd see about that. The gauntlet had been thrown down and I was just the alpha to take up the challenge and prove myself right.

.

Chapter Ten

Justine

A sense of languor set in, my limbs so relaxed that I lay half-sprawled on the missing bedcovers. Our lovemaking had left the room in complete disarray, everything mussed to the nines...just like it should be when the body was allowed free rein.

I listened to Logan in the shower, too tired to join him. Then I remembered the unusual artifact I had found in the prop room. Excitement stirred in my belly, so intense that I jumped out of bed and headed into the bathroom to join him.

When I climbed in behind him, he grinned at me. "Need more, my incorrigible angel?"

I had intended just to ask him about the artifact, but seeing him there, all freshly scrubbed man flesh, the idea completely slipped my mind. I breathed in his heady fragrance and allowed the water to stream over my body. The shower felt good, softening all the overused flesh.

I thought we'd go straight to it, but instead, Logan surprised me. He began to minister to me, filling his hands with shampoo and applying it to my hair, then working up a lather. Rinsing it away, he attended to my body next, paying special attention to all the naughty bits. I grinned as he slipped his soapy fingers between my legs. The massage reheated my lust and I groaned as he brought me to orgasm for the hundredth time today.

Or at least it felt like we had coupled that many times. I was becoming a sex machine, and I couldn't figure out if this was a good thing or a bad thing. Maybe it didn't matter, as I rode his hand harder.

When I was once again limp as a noodle from another orgasm, he took the time to dry me off before attending to himself. The guy had it going on, no doubt about it. An amazing lover who gave more than he expected to receive in return.

"I think it's time I took you out for a real meal. We need to build up your stamina if you're going to be able to keep this up," he teased, his green eyes lit by that inner fire that so turned me on.

"Think we can keep our hands off each other that long?" I teased back as I let him brush my hair. We still stood in the bathroom, naked, enjoying the view.

"Not if you don't wear any panties at the dinner table."

"Are you telling me, sir, or asking?" I immediately threw in.

"Telling you, angel."

His eyes sparked greener as he loomed over me, his teeth looking longer all of a sudden. Mesmerized, I laid a hand on his chest, feeling his heart pounding away under my hand. He was so alive. *Vital. Amazing.* If I had no other needs, I could see us staying in this room and never leaving, not for anything. How had my view changed so much in such a short period of time? No. This could never be. He had his life while I had mine. *This is just sex, lust. Remember that, Justine.*

"Then I will do as you ask." I flashed him my pearly whites and left the room to find my dress. I could only imagine how all that silk would feel on my naked breasts. And I was not disappointed as I let it slip down my body, my nipples budding tightly from the sensation. Oh boy, I had it bad. But it would pass soon, right? All passion did then I could go about my business as usual. This was a rare gift, one that I shouldn't turn away from too soon. I had always wanted to find a 'sir' I trusted. And I instinctively trusted Logan already. Though he would never commit to a relationship either, he did care about looking after me. That was obvious.

When I looked into the mirror to check myself, I was startled at how good I looked after all the lovemaking. I glowed, like I was also lit by an inner fire. For once I didn't see myself as the stuffy professor, but as a real woman with real needs.

Logan came up behind me and stood tall and gorgeous at my side.

"We do make a beautiful pair," I said.

He leaned down and kissed my neck. "You make us beautiful. You shine with an inner beaty seldom seen. That's why I called you angel on first meeting. You have a halo, an aura about you that drew me in." His hands slipped down my body and he cupped my breasts with his large hands. "No underwear, just like I requested. I won't need to punish you then, for not doing my bidding."

I wantonly reached up and allowed him full access to run his hands over my curves. What would happen if I refused? My stomach turned somersaults. Then a different game would begin, I had no doubt. Would I want to go that far? I wasn't certain of that. In fact, the butterflies might be my body's way of saying no. Then again, in a safe atmosphere, I might be enticed to explore things a bit further.

Something told me I'd never get this chance again. I wasn't known for being spontaneous, instead living my life in rather rigid patterns. But I'd always wanted more, longed for that elusive beat that would make me feel entirely alive. Was this it? I hadn't had this overwhelming sense of being in the moment ever before and it was absolutely wonderful to find myself feeling so alive, like I could take on the world and win.

"As you wished, sir."

"No, I changed my mind."

He reached down and brought the hem of my dress up and over my head, leaving me stark naked.

I watched him stride to the dresser and pull out a bra and panties. Coming back to my side, he had me rest my hand on his shoulder while he tugged the underwear up my legs and into place. Then he fastened the bra around my body, tucking my breasts away.

"I can't have every man ogling you all night. I can't speak for what might happen," he said in a darker tone than he had used up until now.

"You would fight for my honor," I quipped.

"You have no idea, angel, of what I am capable." His eyes sparked green fire, like a dragon before he burned an interloper to cinders.

He slipped the dress back down my body. Yes, he was right. I chanced a glance in the mirror. I still looked good, but not like I shopped at Sluts-R-Us. What had I been thinking? What if a student had seen me dressed like that, or a colleague? Thank goodness Logan had kept his head. Perhaps he had my back more than I realized. The man was full of surprises, more complicated than it appeared at first. That thought actually gave me hope.

"What exactly are you capable of?" I asked, my curiosity piqued.

"I'll share soon. I'd like to get to know you better before I share my deepest, darkest secrets."

The intensity of his expression made me want to know more. "I would have thought two people couldn't get much closer than we've been these past hours." I raised my eyebrows with a knowing come-hither look.

"I want to learn every last thing about you. Right from birth. You up for that?" he asked, his eyes challenging me.

I could well imagine him in centuries past forcing a duel at dawn.

"Well, sure, but maybe not all twenty-nine years tonight? Besides, I've heard tell a woman should keep her secrets too," I teased and pulled away, grabbing my purse and preparing to head out of the room.

If he was keeping secrets, then I would pretend I had a few interesting ones of my own. In reality, I didn't think my life was all that exciting, more like what would be expected of someone desperate to get ahead in a hard world. The most fascinating thing about me was my drive to be remembered as someone who discovered something of importance to the human race or created something that brought immortality. Like *that* would be easy.

"Just wait until we get back. You'll be punished for your disobedience if you don't do my bidding and spill all your secrets to me. Mark my words," he said in his most authoritative voice.

I hid a grin and hurried out into the hallway, enjoying the game immensely. So much so that I had almost forgotten why I had climbed in the shower to begin with. I wanted us to discuss the provenance of the artifact that defied any existing ones I was aware of. Just thinking of it sent excitement through my body, setting my mind onto thoughts of what it exactly was. I would need to translate the hieroglyphics to discover more, if indeed it was real.

"Did you have your people create an ancient relic made to look like it's never been uncovered since it was made by ancient peoples?"

"No, it doesn't ring a bell. Did you find something unusual?" Logan asked as he checked his breast pockets for his cellphone and wallet. He wore an expensive black suit that hung off his magnificent frame like he had a tailor at his beck and call. Well, with his money he probably did.

"I did. And it's very intriguing. If it's real, it's an incredible find. I want to pursue documentation and transcribing of the symbols. Any problem with that?"

"As long as I get my fair share of your time. I want this to continue. You sharing my bed."

"At least until the fire burns out, right?" From the relationships I had been party to, that was bound to happen at some point. Why would this be any different? Plus, this wasn't a relationship but two ships passing in the night, as Marnie would call it.

His expression darkened. "A fire like ours is not going to burn out. Mark my words."

"If you say so, sir."

Chapter Eleven

Logan

The way she said *sir*, in that sweet little girl voice that we both knew was entirely fake made me want to fuck her until I shook all the layers of civilization from both of us. I wanted us raw, the real deal. Until then I would do my part, keep her twisting in the wind until she was entirely mine, her passion laid bare. She had no idea of the true dedication of a fated mate. She came from the human world where such passion was unheard of.

In the animal kingdom, the wolf was king, the animal spirit that would be loyal to the death. I just needed her to be one of us to understand where I was coming from. But how? I needed her permission. And she couldn't be shown who I was, who we were, until she agreed.

I needed a plan.

All through the meal, I dealt with the problem while I watched my angel enjoy herself, eating and teasing me with such enthusiasm that I had a new appreciation for my brothers and their mates. What I had seen as cloying and stifling was proving to be something that offered freedom when embraced. Excitement beyond the ken. The real deal.

"Want to see what I mean?" she asked.

"Excuse me?"

Justine was staring at me, a smile tugging at her lips. "You're not paying attention, are you?"

I picked up her hand and kissed the back of it. "I was so overcome by your loveliness I was rendered speechless."

"Then what did I just ask you?" Her fair eyebrows rose over eyes that glowed as blue as a summer sky.

"If I wanted to visit the prop room." My mind had thankfully registered the question even as it worked on the problem of how to get Justine into my life permanently.

"Well, do you?"

"Sure. Shall we?" I asked, getting up and assisting her in leaving her chair.

"A gal could get used to such treatment."

"Good. I want to spoil you. What do you want most in this lifetime?" I asked as we walked side by side out of Niro's.

"Oh, I don't know. I guess to do something that matters. Leave my mark on the world in a positive way."

"You do that now with your teaching. Think of all the students who'll remember you." I kept a close watch as we walked down the hallway to the prop room. I suddenly understood the full weight of being the male partner in a mated relationship—to stay ever alert, to be the protector as well as the provider.

"Hmm, maybe. But I would like to pull back the veil of whatever it is in us that prevents humans from reaching our full potential. Do you know what I mean? I read in so many places that we have no idea of how very much we are capable of, that we never utilize. We use such a small percentage of our brains. That plagues me. Makes me want to do more. Be more. Experience more."

I turned to her and put my hands on her slender shoulders so that she would look me in the eyes. "Would you be willing to change who you are to have that? Give up some of yourself to open yourself to new possibilities that most humans are never aware of in their lifetime?"

"Doesn't all change mean that something is traded for something else?"

"Well said, angel. That's exactly right. Ah, we're here." I opened the door with my key card and shepherded her into the slightly musty space.

"It's over here," she said, hurrying away to point out a large wooden crate she had been working on.

"Smells ancient," I said, joining her after making certain the door closed properly. I didn't like surprises. If anyone learned of the valuable props hidden here, who knew what could happen?

"It does. I hope there are no more spiders." She shuddered and looked around nervously, like she'd just remembered what had occurred earlier. Well, that was one spider I would like to thank—it got her right back into my bed in a timely fashion. Now I just had to hope there would be no more surprises like the twins pulled, to give me time to show her I'd changed and was prepared to step up. Then she would change her mind about being with me. *Us.* I liked the sound of that word. Very much.

"If there are any, I'll take care of it," I assured her.

"My big bad wolf will save me, right?"

"Your big bad wolf would like to do more than save you. Now that I've made certain you're well fed, that is." I grinned like the big bad wolf and caught her smile in return.

"See, the artifact is covered in symbols that need to be transcribed." She pointed at the engravings with enthusiasm.

I peered at what she was pointing at. "That's interesting." Something prickled in the back of my mind.

"I want to start right away on this. If you didn't ask for this to be recreated, then we may have something that's the real deal. Something that will make history."

I shook my head. "I didn't have this made up by the forger, so yeah, it stands a chance of being the real deal."

"Brilliant. I want to get it out of the box and onto a table. If you'll grab the other end—"

"I'll do better than that." I grabbed the silvery-green crystalline object and, surprised it wasn't heavier considering it was almost two meters long and shaped like an ancient sarcophagus, placed it on a long table set up for working on.

"Thanks. I wonder what it's made of? We'll need to test it. I have contacts at the university that could get results fairly quickly. Any problem with my sharing this find with some colleagues?"

"No, I can't imagine that would be an issue. I'm surprised it's made of such thin material and yet appears so strong." I pressed down on it with my hand. "There's a very slight flexible component to it. Strange for an ancient object. They're usually unmalleable."

I began searching for a way to open it up, running my hands over the surface, looking for a crack or a line in the material. I pressed at different spots with the palm of my hand, feeling slight indentations.

Suddenly the object glowed, like the inside had some kind of electric current running through it, then just as quickly dimmed.

"What was that?" Justine's voice held awe at having caught the exact same moment as I had.

"I'm not certain. But there must be a way in."

"You know, there is a legend." Justine's eyes took on a faraway look. "Of an artifact called the Infinity Egg. It's said to be otherworldly. Part of the ancient astronaut theory, but it's most likely a hoax. It will need to be tested first to bring us any answers."

"There's a barely discernible line running around the entire perimeter, like two halves of a coffin."

"I can't wait to X-ray it, see if there's anything inside. I'm tagging it the Infinity Egg until then. It does have a ring to it."

"I'll have it transported to the university tomorrow for you, if you like?" I suggested. I was more than curious about what tests would reveal.

"I would very much like that. I have a class in the morning, but I'm free at ten thirty and can get a geologist colleague to take a look first thing. I'll text her right now."

There was an awkward silence. I knew what I was thinking, but I was more interested in her thoughts. I pulled out my phone and groaned at the number of emails that needed answering as well.

"Looks like playtime is over," she teased, glancing at me for a split second as I began to swipe through the messages, searching for the most urgent ones.

"I wish we were going on vacation right now, not needing to work." My words took me by surprise. I had been thrilled to make a movie and now I wanted to abandon it all to spend time with Justine? That could not be. I needed to pull myself together. We'd still have our nights together and our time on set. Surely that would be enough? But I didn't feel comfortable having her out of my sight for some reason.

I texted Lachlan, checking if it was normal, then sped off a second text to security, asking that they watch out for her when she was away from the Glitter Palace, solving one problem on the spot. No need for hired thugs inside the Glitter Palace run by fellow shifters and filled with clan members.

Lachlan got back to me immediately with a smug emoji and a short message making me wish I hadn't bothered texting him. But his words rang true. What I was experiencing was all completely normal for a Forever Mating, though his final zinger left me concerned. How much more of this would I have to endure before she was mine forever?

Ha! I won the bet. More proof positive, bro. Prepare yourself.

"I should be going," she said. "I have to get up early in the morning."

Perhaps she was right. She was a major distraction. And I still had a lot to prove, both to her and the world. The last twenty-four hours with my angel had made me a different man — a better man. I just needed to follow the fates and do the work.

"I'll take you," I said. I was curious about how she lived. What did she surround herself with?

I grabbed her hand and we abandoned the room, checked the door was locked and headed for the lobby.

"Would you bring my car around, please," I instructed my personal concierge at the door.

"Of course, sir."

The *sir* made Justine's lips quirk up in a slight grin. I relished it, thinking ahead to all the wonders yet to be. I suppressed them instantly when the mere thought made me hard. Maybe there would be time for lovemaking at her place?

The flashy red Lamborghini was brought quickly up to the curb and I assisted her inside. Why not spend money on the fun things? No matter what, I would never give up enjoying the best life has to offer. And my angel looked so beautiful surrounded by finer things, as she should always be. No, *would* always be from now on. I looked forward to all the things my money would buy. What good was it if not to be spent making a loved one happy?

"Where do you live?" I asked, then plugged in the information she revealed to the satnav.

We sped off into the star-filled night and she gave a squeal that turned into a happy grin as we raced down the Vegas Strip.

"It corners like it's on rails!" she exclaimed, her excitement catching. She looked so young, so carefree at that moment that I wanted to hug her. Instead, I paid careful attention to my driving, making certain she was safe and protected.

"Want to come in?" she asked as I pulled into her driveway ten minutes later. She lived in the suburbs, in a small detached house that reminded me of a cottage back home. She should live in a castle, or a manor house at the very least. But the property was well maintained and the neighborhood was safe, from what I could observe. Of course, I would have a report on my desk by morning.

"Of course, angel. I want to see how you live."

I helped her out of the low seat, enjoying the feel of taking her hand in mine. Every time we touched, electricity leaped between us, making a vibrating circuit that heightened the moment. The world seemed more alive, filled with promises that glowed in the dark.

Once we were inside her home, she turned on a few lights. "Can I get you anything to drink?"

I gathered her into my arms, renewed once more with having her close, her heart beating in tandem with my own. Things were moving so quickly, at lightning speed. But I had heard of this from my brothers. *That once you're thunderstruck, there's no going back.*

A loud knock on the outside door brought me back to the real world.

"Who could that be?" Justine pulled away and went to check through the peephole. "Brad?" she said in some surprise as she opened the door.

Who in the hell is Brad?

The man who stood on the top step looked distressed, his eyes reddened by emotion. Shorter than me and with pale, washed-out coloring, we stared at one another for a second before he turned away.

"I'm sorry. You have company. I just…needed to talk to someone." Even his voice was weak. No wonder she needed me.

"What is it, Brad?"

Damn, my angel was concerned. I could hear the empathy in her tone. Of course she would be. She was an angel, after all. Even at inconvenient times.

"It's Mother. She's in the hospital. She took a spill today. Broke her hip."

"*Oh my God*, is she going to be okay?" Justine asked.

I inwardly groaned. Just who were Brad and his mother to Justine? I sensed he might have been more than a friend showing up out of the blue. Damn, he'd better be an ex and not a current boyfriend. My inner wolf began to prowl, howling to be released to deal with things. Let Brad know Justine had a new man and he would appreciate Brad not calling after the sun went down. Or after the sun rose, if he knew what was good for him.

"Would you like to come in?" Justine asked, opening the door wider.

"I don't want to put you out…"

Then don't.

"It's okay. I'm sure Logan will understand. Brad Smith, meet Logan Creig. He's here in town to direct the filming of a movie. I've been hired by him to assist with the artifacts that will be stolen in the heist. But you don't want to hear about that. Please, have a seat. I'll fix you some tea? Coffee?"

"Just water, please. It's late for stimulants."

A damn wuss. I knew it. He didn't even bother to try for a handshake.

"I'll have a whiskey. Whatever you have is fine," I said, sitting down on the sofa and making a point of looking completely comfortable, not taking my eyes off the interloper for one second.

"Straight up?"

I nodded.

Justine left to get our drinks and I began the interrogation immediately. "So, what is it you do, *Brad*?" I exaggerated the use of his name.

He glanced at me nervously and perched on a straight-backed chair, smoothing down his thinnish no-color hair. "I work in the university library, buying and recording inventory for students and staff alike."

"The library?" I raised my eyebrows with some disdain. *Figures, he looks like a person who hides away in the dark.* I'd bet he still lived in his mother's basement. Of course, technically, I lived with The Creig. But, all of us owned Castle Creigbourne, plus we had our own wings, so it was like comparing apples and oranges. Or in this case, alphas and weaklings.

"Here we go." Justine was back. She handed me a snifter of fragrant whiskey and Brad-boy a bottle of water. She appeared nervous and I didn't like the vibe she was giving off one bit. I took my eyes off the pair for a second to text my man to check up on this Brad Smith, adding the few facts I knew already. I couldn't very well ask the boy for his middle name—it would have seemed a tad out of place.

I sipped my whiskey while Brad's story spilled out. How he'd found his mother on the kitchen floor early in the morning and had called nine-one-one. What it had been like in the hospital. At one point he looked to Justine, his expression and voice extra whiny, and asked why she didn't answer his texts. All he needed was the world's tiniest violin playing to complete the picture.

"I'm sorry about what happened to your mom, but we're not together now. We haven't talked in months. I was busy and didn't look at my phone for hours." She blushed at the revelation.

Of course she was busy – she was with me. In my bed and calling me sir. Where we should be right now, Braddy.

"That's okay. You weren't to know." Brad sat up a bit straighter and sipped at his water. *Generous of him.* My wolf growled. Then Brad glanced at me as I stared at him. "So, you're directing a movie?"

"Yes, at the Glitter Palace."

"Does that mean you put up your own money?" he asked, if somehow that would taint the experience by making it a vanity project. I'd run into this deplorable attitude before.

"Of course. I'm also one of the executive producers. If I don't believe in it enough to put up my own money, then why should I make it? Or ask others to put up any cash?"

Brad frowned. Maybe the guy was a bit dim. His next question surprised and annoyed me.

"Is the casting couch still a thing?" Brad had finally perked up, as if maybe this zinger would do the trick. *Passive-aggressive asshole.*

"Not in my film. I can't speak for Hollywood. Good guys and *assholes* everywhere. They even hide out in libraries." I made sure to send him a solid stare as I used the word asshole, to confirm I meant him.

"Can I talk to you in the kitchen, Logan?"

Sure. You want me to get rid of him for you, angel? I'm your guy.

Chapter Twelve

Justine

"I hope you understand, Logan, but I need to spend a little time with Brad, reassuring him. He's pretty upset and your presence is only upsetting him more. You're like...too much for him to handle in the state he's in."

"I'm not leaving you alone with a strange man." Logan crossed his arms over his chest, his expression turning defiant. "I don't trust him."

"What! Brad? The guy's harmless. He couldn't harm a flea."

"Who is he to you?"

"An old boyfriend. We broke up months ago as I already mentioned. He was too close to his mother, I thought. But I didn't see this coming. Poor guy." I spoke as quietly as possible, not wanting Brad to overhear.

Then Brad lurched into the kitchen, his face so pale it appeared bloodless.

I rushed to his side to support him. "What's wrong? Is it your mother?"

"I have to go. She's taken a turn for the worse. She just texted me."

"I'll drive you. You're in no shape."

"No. I'll drive him," Logan said, his voice like steel, dismissive of any interference.

Brad gave me a pitiful look and I knew what it meant. Logan scared him. He wanted me to drive him. A compromise was in order. At that moment I understood the dynamics of the situation. I could refuse Logan's help, but then I was really asking for the man I wanted to be my *sir* to be someone he could never be. Plus, would I really want Logan's ex-girlfriend to show up and need his help?

I might have looked like an angel to Logan, but I wasn't. I did have a jealous streak that I made no apologies for. We might have spent only one day together, most of it having wild, incredible sex that had changed my expectations going forward on a fundamental level of what was possible in the bedroom, but I think I already knew enough about uber-alpha men to say that much at least. That they didn't go for other men hanging around their women. Even if said woman was only with them for a short while.

Because obviously, this couldn't last. We'd combust in the bedroom at some point and become nothing but stardust. I nearly laughed inappropriately at the idea, swallowing my discomfort with a hiccup.

"Let's all go. A show of concern from all of us will only help your mom," I said, certain I had played the hand dealt with aplomb.

"But he doesn't know my mother," Brad complained, his reddened eyes shooting pitiful darts at Logan.

"Let's go. I'm driving," Logan said and strode from the room. I gave Brad a nod as he grumbled under his breath and we all headed out into the night.

A stressful trip to the hospital was an understatement. Brad whimpered in the back seat while Logan looked like a warrior on a mission, his expression rock hard behind the wheel. I kept my cool, watching the colorful flow of images slide by the window, all aglitter with showy Vegas neon lights and flashy images.

Logan pulled to a vigorous stop in the hospital parking lot then stalked around to open my door for me.

"Ever the gentleman," I teased quietly as he assisted me from the vehicle.

"When in the presence of an angel, it is the correct modus operandi," he said far more loudly than me, adding a respectful nod of his head. Brad groaned aloud for attention as he lumbered from the back seat.

Yeah, I can call things. Men.

We entered the hospital entrance, the doors whooshing shut behind us. The bright glare of the overhead lights only brought more attention to Brad's mottled expression. *Poor man.* He was really suffering, his whole world hanging in the balance. He loved his mom so much and I respected him for it. But it left very little room for another woman in his life, as I had learned the hard way. I was okay with that. *Now.*

And truly, I needed a man who was more in charge. Maybe I had a thing for bad boys? Just thinking of Logan riled up enough to want to do delicious things to me under the sheets had the blood pounding in my brain. *Ah, the brain.* The biggest sex organ of them all, according to scientific research.

Big question was, how far did I want this submissive and Dom scenario to go? Did I want to be spanked? Punished for being a bad little girl? Maybe just a little, ease into it by dipping my big toe in the water. But not so far that I couldn't control things. Then I did laugh out loud, gaining odd looks from both men havering at my sides as we took the elevator to the fourth floor. Control was the one thing a sub was supposed to give over, right?

In efforts to stall my raging libido — after all we were in a hospital — I directed my thoughts to the fascinating artifact I'd unearthed today. I needed to keep my decorum and thinking about the object I was going to research at my leisure was certainly the way to go. What did the strange symbols represent? In all my time studying Egyptian history, I had never come across the exact ones carved into the Infinity Egg. If they were real, history was about to be made. Almost as exciting a scenario as getting back into bed with Logan. *Damn, there I go again.*

As if he could read my mind, Logan gave me what only could be called a wolfish look, his face all planes and angles, hungry, like he wanted to pounce on me. My nipples tightened almost painfully while my pussy clenched with a growing need around a very unsatisfying empty sensation. *Breathe.*

He leaned down and whispered one riveting word into my ear, warming my skin with the closeness of his lips. "Later."

I nodded, certain that someone else inhabited my body. Someone who just couldn't get enough of him. Someone who wanted to fuck him silly until the sun came up again. Maybe we could find an empty room somewhere. Just share a quickie to tide us over? Doctors and nurses did that, right? Patients too, I'd bet, knowing the human animal.

I glanced up at Logan as the elevator dinged before opening its doors. His well-formed and talented lips were curved upward, like he was enjoying himself now. Almost like he could sense my arousal. Well, maybe he could. I certainly knew he was hard, noting how he needed to arrange himself as discreetly as possible.

The three of us continued to tramp down the hallway, headed for the hospital room we'd been directed to by a nurse. At the doorway, Logan and I hung back, waiting for Brad to go inside and speak with his mom. Surprisingly, she was sitting up in bed, looking sprightly, greeting her son with a smile. Not bad for a woman who just broke her hip. My respect for her grew at that moment.

"Brad, thank goodness you're here. I need you to get a few things for me at the gift shop. Ah, you've brought visitors," she said looking past her son to note us hovering at the doorway. *This was her emergency?*

She was playing games again, I thought, remembering how often she would call Brad home to deal with some major problem that could have easily waited. I mean, not be able to find the remote for the TV, accusing him of hiding it? And the woman has all her faculties—she'd been tested. Sharp as a tack. Not to mention the occasion she'd interrupted demanding he look for the TV remote had been Valentine's Day. I didn't think I was far wrong in calling this one what it was. *No-woman-good-enough-for-her-son syndrome.*

Introductions were quickly made and the older woman perked up at the information of what Logan was in town for. Apparently, she was a *big* fan of movies. She had a lot of questions for him and he stood at her bedside, quietly and patiently answering all her inquiries. I liked that, though I wanted to get him alone soon. I pressed my thighs tightly together in efforts to suppress my growing need.

"We should be going, Mrs. Smith," Logan said, picking up her hand and gallantly kissing the back of it. "You need your rest."

"Call me Mabel, all my friends do." Mabel flirted with a preening hand busy fluffing at her hair, arranging a few silver curls across her forehead. *Mabel.* Huh, in the few weeks Brad and I had been dating, I'd only known her as Mrs. Smith.

"Mabel it is." God, he had a sexy voice, all low timbre and throaty. It made a woman think of dim lights and sexy maneuvers. Good thing this was just short term. Too much of this man could be downright addictive.

"Lovely woman," Logan remarked as we made our way from the room after Brad assured us that he'd take an Uber home.

"Indeed."

He smirked at me. "What? You don't agree?"

"Yes, she's fine. Just a bit needy and hard on her son."

"Tell me about Brad." His voice instantly hardened, like Brad was his nemesis.

"Not much to say really. We only dated a few weeks and weren't right for each other."

"Because of his mother?"

"Not only that. He was a bit…shall we say…not as confident in who he was as he could be." I glanced up at Logan, noting he was paying close attention to my answers. I liked that. He truly did want to know more about me as a person. Our connection, intense and visceral, so immediate, seemed much more than it should be. Dare I say, on another level? I hesitated to name it, afraid it was real, it felt rather…mystical. Destined, like our being together was welcomed by the universe. *A passing insanity, no doubt.*

"You want a man to take charge?" His eyes smoldered like we were headed to the bedroom this very moment.

I swallowed, my mouth filling with saliva, my pussy just as wet. "Sometimes," I whispered.

We were near his vehicle now and he pressed the key fob, helping me into the front seat.

"I need you now, angel, like I need my next breath," he said with complete and utter sincerity, his voice roughed by deep emotion. Any other man saying such words would not have been believable. But with Logan it was different. And I knew that need, more than I cared to admit.

Chapter Thirteen

Logan

I reached over and drew her to me, rougher than I intended. Took that beautiful face between the palms of my hands and claimed a kiss of those perfect pink lips. The effect was startling, satisfying, essential, the electrical current between us bursting into the hottest flames.

I pressed harder, seeking the warmth within. My blood was on fire, coursing under my skin, tightening my cock until it felt about to burst free from my pants, hard as steel. A moan. A gasp. The outside world dropped away, making only this moment, this second, all that mattered.

She softened into me across the annoyance of the center partition between the seats. I wanted to drag her right up close to me, push into her, fill her with myself. I was lost in her, grasping a full breast and finding the nipple hard, budded. The warmth of the pliant flesh sent me reeling. God, I wanted her. Wanted to have her stretched naked beneath me, wet for only me. Wanted into the very core of her. To make me forget who we are and where we are.

"Fuck, woman," I murmured against her lips. "I have to have you. Now. I can't wait." Our breaths mingled, heating the air around us, obscuring the outside world as moisture formed, clouding over the windows. It ran down the glass in rivets, hiding us from the world.

I pulled at her clothing until she began to help me, shucking off her shoes and panties in one frantic movement. I unbuckled my belt and pulled down the zipper, then yanked another condom from my pocket. I would need to buy more — we'd gone through so many today.

She tore it from my hands and before I could get my pants and boxers completely off, she was on top of me, centering herself over me, grasping my cock with one hand, rolling the condom on and thrusting me into her pussy. I slid inside, pushing past the slick, tight entrance to thrust up into her, pulling her down as far as I could, burying myself balls-deep inside her tight warmth. Life-affirming, in all its haunting magic.

"Oh, my God," I moaned, my cock straining for sweet release, my head swimming with the quickness of being inside her. I lunged into her, burying my face in her fragrant hair, working my hands over her naked breasts, pushing her bra cups down to make them jut out farther until she moaned against my mouth, wetness flooding her channel.

My body wasn't my own, my need too powerful. I forgot everything else, where we were, what was going on. I was rough, rougher than I had ever been with a woman. My hot cum rushed up from inside my balls, tingling and seeking release. Raw. Like I had never known. Harder than I had ever been.

"I'm coming—" I growled, tugging on her nipples, reaching down and rubbing on her swollen clit, wanting her to reach orgasm with me.

I sucked one tightly budded nipple into my mouth, drawing hard and eliciting more sweet moans. I took a deep breath, my lungs about to burst as I forgot to breathe. The fragrance of sex filled the vehicle, our odors mingling.

"I'm almost there," she shouted, slamming herself down on to me over and over, her breasts bouncing with each impact, her pussy squeezing me tight. A final thrust and we collapsed against each other, into each other, breath harsh and resounding in the confining space.

An alarm went off nearby, blasting through the thick, moisture-laden air. I reached around my angel and turned off the offending electronics, the action causing her reddened breasts to press up against my chest. I felt her heartbeat, precious life coursing through her body, sending signals right back down to my cock. *Sweet Jesus, help me*, I wanted her again. *Right now.* I grabbed hold of myself with great difficulty, coming out of the madness that had descended. What the hell had I been thinking? In a parking lot like a pair of teenagers? "We need to go home and do this upright."

She looked at me, the same height as me on my lap. Her eyes searched mine, their depths bluer and the gold speckles shining. Her honesty shone through, seeking to touch my soul. She swallowed, the moment suspended as the lights and stars blinked and danced around us. I wanted to kiss my way down that slim column again, kiss every square inch of her again. In a proper bed this time.

"Yes," she said with a nod.

We raced through the night, everything brighter around us, our bodies in tune with each and every discovery of the other. How on earth could I ever let this woman go? I had to persuade her we were meant to be. That this was not just happenstance, but the real deal.

I pulled up in her driveway and turned off the car. Without another word, we headed inside. We were in mutual agreement that we would spend this night together.

"Would you like a drink?" she asked as soon as I closed the front door, locking it against the world.

"You were a bad girl tonight, my naughty angel, letting me fuck you in plain view of others," I said, testing the waters. I knew on some level she wanted the real me to bring out the real her. I wanted to do this right, find the balance, but my needs were pushing all common sense aside.

She blushed. "I was. Are you going to punish me, Logan?"

Her coyness was my undoing. I grabbed her hands and pinned them up over her head, her body open and languid to my view. My cock. I pressed against her to let her feel how hard her words had made me.

I tore off her dress and her underwear, exposing her. She still smelled of me, our odors mingled in her body. I wanted more than that. My wolf wanted it just as badly. To mark her, claim her as ours so that my scent could never be washed off.

"You don't know what you're asking of me. I can't always control this thing. I'm too alpha. I might overstep, cause you pain that I wouldn't want you to endure," I warned her.

"You could never hurt me. That much I already know," she said, her eyes shining brightly, her body amazing in the low light, all curves and sweet spots.

"Don't be so sure," I said, my body overheating now. My wolf roamed the edges of the room, pressing for advantage. *For the final score.*

"I can take it." Her words taunted me.

"No, you can't," I said, shaking my head with reluctance. She really had no idea who I was, what I was capable of. "I should go. There's so much you don't know about me. Maybe I can soon tell you." Right. *Like if by chance you become one of us which is not likely to happen anytime soon.*

"Tell me now," she insisted.

I wanted to. Tell her everything, what I am, what this all meant. But I couldn't. It went against all the things the Wulvers stand for. We must hide our existence from the world — at our peril we exposed ourselves.

But I also couldn't leave her. Never had I known that such a powerful force in the universe existed. One that would defy all common sense, all sense of what is right and wrong. She was my other half. The part long missing that suddenly made my entire life make sense. My Forever Mate.

Chapter Fourteen

Justine

On my third cup of DEFCON level five coffee in efforts to pry my eyes open after another incredible night spent in such passionate lovemaking that I'd managed *maybe* ten winks, I navigated the long hallways of the university toward the office I shared with another professor. My phone rang just as I unlocked the door and I fumbled with my briefcase and cup, barely managing to juggle everything.

I let out a loud sigh of exasperation and set my stuff down to answer Marnie.

"Morning, m'matey. Thought I'd check in and see how your interview went with the director before starting to drill some teeth."

A big yawn inadvertently escaped. "Already morning, is it?"

"You don't sound very alert. Another late night?"

"Yup. But it was worth it." Just thinking of last night had me heated all over again. It was as if some kind of insanity had entered my system that being in the sack seemed to ease. Maybe I was at that time of the month when a woman was most fertile and my body instinctively thought Logan an excellent candidate for the perfect genetic material? Good thing we had used protection then. The last thing I needed was to get pregnant from a man who could never go the distance, as much as I wanted children one day. But there had to be some reason for this insane attraction.

"Was it the same guy who you met at the wedding?"

"Yup. And this is going to come as a big shock…he's also the director of the movie."

"What! You're kidding, right? That's some coincidence. So, you're banging the director? Sounds like the casting couch still exists," she teased.

"I would have gotten the job without having sex with Logan. It wasn't like that." Defensive now, I took another big sip of the coffee. That was two people who had recently mentioned the casting couch to me, which reminded me. "Brad came by last night. His mother's in the hospital recovering from a fall. She was doing fine when we visited last night, thank goodness."

Marnie gave a low whistle. "How did all that go?'

"Logan drove us all to the hospital to help out."

"That was good of him. Then he spent the night?"

"Right again."

"I'm not certain if I should say anything—"

"You can tell me anything. You know that," I said, plunking down in my office chair.

"Be careful. Wild sex for a night or two is one thing, but keep it up and the heart gets involved. For us females, anyway."

I snorted. "I think my heart knows better than to take chances with any man." I had to admit though, her words struck a chord. I should pull back on the reins soon. Well, today was a weeknight, so I'd prove I was capable and head straight home after working on the set at the casino. *Prove I'm more than capable of protecting myself.*

"Good hearts get women in trouble all the time. We think we can fix a man, get him to turn one hundred and eighty degrees around to the right side. Never works, in any relationship I've ever been introduced to. How many orgasms have you had?"

"Too many to count, but that's not the point." My phone pinged to remind me of an appointment. "I gotta go. Work's calling."

"Just be careful, that's all I ask."

"No problem, skipper," I said in my most cheerful of tones and ended the call.

Excitement began building as I hurried from my office to the lab where the Infinity Egg had been brought this morning. My fatigue quite forgotten, I pushed open the door and took a look around the space. Chrome, long metal tables, calibrated machines and paraphernalia greeted me, while the artifact to be studied sat on prominent display in the center of the room.

"Morning, Professor," Professor Cynthia Dixon greeted me with a smile, wearing a lab coat with her hands enclosed in rubber gloves as she looked over at me.

I murmured a greeting and hurried to join her. "What do you think it's made of?"

"Excellent question. It's quite remarkable. So lightweight, yet so strong. I'm not certain at the moment. I'll need to conduct a series of tests this morning. I should have some answers fairly soon, maybe by lunchtime. But first, it needs a good, careful cleaning. All the symbols are encased with dirt and grime making it impossible to tell what is written all over it. That should prove fascinating in itself. That's your field, right? Egyptology."

"Hmm. Okay, I'll be back in a couple of hours. I've got a class to teach now."

I scurried back down the halls to the lecture theater. The class went well enough, considering my lack of sleep, and finally I was free to get back to the lab. My curiosity was making me antsy by the time the last student had exited the room.

I burst through the lab door five minutes later. "So, what did you learn?"

Cynthia looked up from her laptop she was busy keyboarding at. She shook her head. "You're not going to believe this. It's an amazing result. I've run the tests three times to make sure there was no error. But wow, this is *not* what I was expecting at all."

Cynthia's face was bright with excitement, a state I seldom saw in the teaching staff, I was sorry to report.

"Tell me!"

"The material or alloy this artifact is made of, I'm one hundred percent certain it's not of earthly origin."

"What? That's impossible!"

"I've ruled out everything it could be before coming to this conclusion. I don't take it lightly, Professor."

"Of course! Sorry if it sounded like I doubted you." I smoothed the waters.

The large coffin-shaped object was now clean and shiny, brilliant in the overhead lighting. It did indeed look more otherworldly than before. All the symbols were revealed now, riveting me. I ran my fingertips lightly over them. They all represented animals or species, most of which I had never known to exist on Earth.

The blood dripping from a fang...did that represent vampires? And the huge white-furred bipedal creature, was that supposed to be the mysterious yeti? A huge wolf-like creature, meant to represent werewolves no doubt, drew my eye as well. What the hell! There were at least a hundred symbols, representing a vast field of primates, ungulates, aquatic, carnivorans, canines, marsupials, reptiles and even bovines.

Confused, I asked, "Is there anything inside?"

She shook her head. "Nothing was picked up by any of our instruments or technology. But there could be. I can't say for certain."

"Well, I really don't know what to say or think about this. I have no experience with anyone having found such a thing."

"I'd say it was a hoax, except, how could it be? It's made of something I can't identify. It makes no sense. It's a quandary. A true mystery."

Observing the universal symbol for mankind, I pressed my palm down on the slight indentation. The object began to brighten. But instead of just glowing for a split second like last night, it continued to shine before the egg cracked open a few centimeters and a beam of light escaped. It coalesced into a swirling hologram image about a foot away from the crack. A bright star shape appeared, hovering above the table.

Stunned, I could only stare at it. Discordant notes erupted from the floating image, pure gibberish to my ears. Was it a language I didn't know? I knew several, but this went beyond my knowledge.

"Speak English, please," I pleaded. *As if that would ever happen.* But I was desperate to know what the hologram implanted inside the device was trying to communicate. It sounded important.

"A member of the Homo sapiens, humankind, of which there are forty-nine million, one hundred and seventeen thousand and thirty-three on planet Earth. Amenemope, son of Psusennes I, reigns in Egypt at present date, 1001 BC."

The star suddenly stopped talking, the light dimmed then it retracted back inside the object, like it had never happened.

"What the heck was that?" Cynthia let out a whoosh of breath.

"I have no idea." My mind worked furiously at the puzzle. "But I think we may have just discovered the missing link. I pressed down on the human image and got this read out in English once it knew what I wanted! Crazy, definitely. But if that can occur for humans, what happens if one presses the other images?"

With bated breath, I lay the palm of my hand on one of the other engraved symbols. Nothing happened. Not even a slight stir. Was this because I represented human beings and the one my hand hovered over was of a legendary creature, not actually seen on Earth except by an eccentric few?

"Lay your hand on the human symbol," I encouraged Cynthia.

She did, her expression rapt.

The egg instantly obliged, opening up once more to give us the short spiel from the glittering star. Scientists would be pleased to hear their projections of our population on Earth were darn close to what the hologram image was reporting.

"*Fascinating.* What culture could have created such a remarkable item?" Cynthia asked with wide eyes, her entire appearance changed in the past few minutes. It did indeed seem like we had witnessed a miracle.

I shook my head. "None that I know of. If this is truly as ancient as it is proving to be, then we have to ask — is it for real? And if so, can it identify other species that touch it in the proper spot? Is this meant to be a historical means of leaving a legacy?"

"You mean the supernatural creatures it's engraved with? That's not possible. There are no werewolves, vampires, angels and demons running around everywhere that I know of. This has *got* to be a hoax!" Cynthia looked two parts horrified and one part fascinated with the idea.

"Yeah, if only we knew a real werewolf — imagine finding out what the oracle might say then!" I grinned at the audacious idea.

"But it's not made of a known earthly substance. That's what's bothering me the most," Cynthia confessed.

"We need to bring other specialists in on this."

Her eyes narrowed. "And give up this opportunity? I think not. Too soon to share this anyway. I need to make copious notes, record all my findings first before we even begin to consider letting others know. I don't want my reputation ruined by saying this is the real deal then having someone find out something that proves it not."

"But can't we avoid that by saying we just want to confer, like I'm doing with you?" I pointed out an easier position to defend.

"And have someone else steal the thunder! You know what these 'hallowed halls' are like. No, I think not. But right now, I want to photograph the response to stimuli. Can you lay your hand in the correct position again?" Cynthia asked.

"Of course."

We had just completed the task when the lab door flew open and in strode the dean, his suit straining to contain his outrage.

"Why aren't you on set, Professor Bell? You should be on set," Dean 'Two-Times' Thornton asked, getting right down to business, his bow tie quivering with indignation.

"I just finished teaching a class this morning and was conferring with Professor Dixon," I explained. "I discussed all this with Logan—Mr. Creig, the film director. I'll be heading there shortly."

"There's been a change of plans. Professor Ledger will be taking over your classes until the movie is completed. Apparently, you now have a part in said movie and you're needed on set all day. Well done, well done. This bodes excellently for the university."

Anger fueled my outrage. What was this? Now I was supposed to hang around the set all day, wasting time when I should be teaching young minds? Or helping in the lab? Hell, even marking papers beat that.

Though on second thoughts, if I brought a laptop along, I could work on my book between shots…surely I could find a quiet corner? Or maybe they had rented RVs for actors? Not that my role was much, maybe not large enough to warrant special treatment. Thornton had a hard-on for the movie, so no point in complaining. Tenure beckoned with open arms if I could keep my shit together.

"What's this?" Dean Thornton asked, coming closer to observe the Infinity Egg.

Cynthia glanced at me and gave a slight shake of her head.

"Just something that's being refurbished for the movie set. Cynthia was kind enough to clean it up. It's going back there now."

"I'll have campus security help you carry it out." The dean pulled out his phone and barked the order into it before either Cynthia or I could stop him. I could see the horror in her eyes, and I grimaced with sympathy. But I couldn't very well object now.

"Fascinating piece. Fascinating. But it really doesn't look at all period. Are you approving this artifact for the movie, Professor?" Dean Thornton asked. He moved closer and ran his hands around.

Oh, God, please don't set it off!

"I think it's meant to be a surprise. An object of unknown origin." I shrugged. "I was careful to suggest it's definitely not true to the era. The set has many beautiful pieces that are absolute duplicates of known artifacts. You should see the death mask of Tut. The director had it made from real gold."

Dean Thornton's eyes grew wide in his pudgy face. "Really? That would cost a fortune today. I must drop by the set soon. You can introduce me to your castmates."

Oh Lord, just strike me dead now! I nodded with as much enthusiasm as I could muster. Two strapping men from campus security came barreling in the room at that moment.

"You called us, Professor Thornton?" one asked.

"Ah, good, good. Would you see to it that this prop is taken to the Glitter Palace immediately? You can follow Professor Bell in your vehicle."

With no choice but to allow it to happen, I gave the two men directions then ushered them out the door, holding it wide for them to carry the Infinity Egg carefully through. Not likely that it could be harmed though, because surely something so important would be made of indestructible, if unknown alloys? My last brief glance as the door swung closed was of Cynthia's stricken expression. Poor woman, just as she had something so unbelievable in her clutches, it had been torn away from her. Somehow, I had to make it up to her. But another part of me was glad to get it back to Logan. I didn't want to be responsible if something happened to such a valuable, impossible-to-replace asset.

Fifteen minutes later, we arrived at the casino. I jumped out of my vehicle and directed the removal of the egg from the campus SUV into the lobby by the security detail, then down the hallway to the prop room.

The halls were teeming with people and we had to make our way awkwardly around small groups. Some there to gamble, others there to meet someone for lunch or perhaps because the first shots of the movie were scheduled for today and they wanted to see what was going on.

Even I felt some excitement stirring at seeing a shoot close up. Though not nearly as much as the thought of seeing Logan again. Last night had even beaten out the first night with a new record number of orgasms. *Keep this up and I should be studied myself!* I also longed to share what was now known about the Infinity Egg with Logan, wanting desperately to see how he'd react to putting his own hand on the pictograph for human and observing the artifact do its amazing act.

Inside the prop room, I gestured at a large table. "Please, just set it there."

The Infinity Egg was duly deposited in place and the two men excused themselves.

"We'll take a look around, if that's okay with you, Professor?" one asked.

I shrugged. "Why not? Others are."

As the door closed behind them, I laid my hands back on the intriguing egg. It called to me on an elemental level. I've been on some pretty inspiring digs in my time, discovering some wonderful ancient items, but this one, this artifact, beat all.

I checked the time. I should hurry and catch up with the film crew in Nero's, the location they were working in today, but I hated to leave the egg alone. Well, the door was secure. And only I and Cynthia knew of the item's importance. The golden death mask of Tut was a more likely target, if it came to that. Just like in his movie, *The Vegas Job*.

Logan had had a good idea, setting his heist in a casino. Sin City was prime for such shenanigans. It had even been built by the mob back in the day. Crime bosses like Bugsy Seigel running the Flamingo or Moe Dalitz of the famed Desert Inn, who got his start by taking over another person's investment. Not an uncommon occurrence.

Double checking the prop room door was properly secure, I turned around to the corridor...and caught sight of a man dressed in black, right down to his shiny shoes and hair color. I'd just been thinking about gangsters, and this guy's striking resemblance to John Gotti, with his polished looks, made me stop mid-action. The tough guy was scoping me out, I was sure of it. Should I go back inside? I was running late as it was. But then the man was joined by another man, one who looked far less threatening.

In fact, this second man, short in stature and with a mild, almost conciliatory manner, held out a pamphlet or brochure to the man in black. The big guy took it without squawking. To my surprise, they began to chat, the small man's expression one of intense earnestness as he waved his arms about, trying to be persuasive. He appeared elated, like he was sharing the very best news possible, making me want to eavesdrop. Thoughts of Vegas's history with the mob had been playing on me, but this was something else entirely. I moved in closer to listen, although it wasn't like they were trying to hide their conversation or anything, their voices loud.

"You're saying this group, Creation's Witnesses, is able to see the future? Has the power to change things for the better and is on the verge of obtaining life-changing knowledge that will assist all of mankind. Those are some pretty big claims to be making, buddy," the man in black said with a shake of his head. But his expression gave the game away. He was intrigued, the same as me. *Hmm*. The name Creation's Witnesses did not ring a bell. Who were they?

"You're welcome to attend our next meeting. See for yourself. Share a meal and a musical interlude with us and listen to our prophet, Jane Wheaton. Then if you're not satisfied that we can do as we claim, we'll give *you* a gift just for coming out to visit."

They turned my way and noticed me hovering nearby.

"Young lady, would you be interested in attending one of Creation's Witnesses meetings?" The eager young man held out a folded sheet of paper containing colorful images, his pale eyes myopic.

"Thanks." I automatically accepted his offering. I glanced at the idyllic pictures of happy people in pristine exotic locations as he gave me a similar spiel to the one he'd given to gangster guy.

"The next meeting's tonight. You're more than welcome to join us. Or anytime for that matter, just drop by. We love meeting like-minded people who care about humanity's future. The address is on the brochure."

I smiled back with regret. "Sounds interesting, but I'm afraid all my time is taken for the foreseeable future. Not only do I have a regular job, but I'm moonlighting as a consultant." I wouldn't normally share that much about myself with complete strangers, but the small man looked so keen, so wanting me to attend, I had to let him down easy.

"Do you have a website or a campaign or something that one can donate to?" I could maybe send some money to their cause, if my research discovered it was legit.

"No. We're not into all that modern stuff. Waste of money and planet resources. We're the real deal, doing it as a grassroots movement."

"Excellent. I know what you mean."

"You are *exactly* the kind of person we need. Please, say you'll join us or at least come by and break bread with us?" The smaller man's eyes turned a bit zealous for my comfort. *Not another of those groups that presses too hard, too fast.* He lost me there.

"I wish I could, but I've just got too much on my plate right now. You understand."

"You're either with us or against us," he said, in a chilling tone that took me off guard. He dropped the zealot mask, revealing a dark nature lurking inside him. Like he knew I was never going to show up at their place of business, meaning he had nothing to lose by attacking me. The abrupt change left me spinning.

"You'll need to excuse me," I said stiffly, my back up. What the fuck was he thinking? A terrible way to try to influence anyone.

I threw the brochure in the paper recycling bin and glanced back to see the two men glaring at me. I hurried off, impatient to get to Nero's and forget all about this crazy encounter that had used up precious minutes. Damn, but that guy had fooled me. Angry at myself for being taken in, I increased my step.

Rounding the final corner into the ballroom, I took in the gargantuan space with its expansive ceiling that allowed all sorts of camera equipment and booms to be set up. I stopped inside the doorway to watch the show, impressed in spite of misgivings at having to say some dialogue lines at some future point. Speaking of which, where was my script?

The excitement inside was palpable, and yet very organized with everyone seeming to know exactly what to do at any given second. And at the heart of the action stood Logan Creig. *Oh my, but he looks good today.* Filled with that seething intensity that made his every move so darn watchable, mesmerizing even. I couldn't have looked away even if I'd wanted to. He moved like a predator, each step so perfectly placed, so deliberate, that he commanded the room. He should be starring in the movie. I know I'd watch it over and over again if he did. So would any female with a pulse.

Not wanting to interrupt, I stood on the fringes of the crowd, though I longed to move closer for our glances to meet. Logan moved over to a dolly with a camera and operator, climbed aboard and looked through the lens over the man's shoulder. He gestured at the table of actors he must be preparing to film. The dolly then rose a few feet to get a better angle, pushed by a couple of men.

"Professor Bell! Where have you been? I've been looking all over for you. Here are your lines. We need you in makeup like yesterday. Come with me!" The torrent of words rushed out at me, all spoken by the scriptwriter I had met in Logan's office. What was her name again? Yes, Valerie.

"Sorry, I got here as fast as I could," I said, but I was speaking to her back as she dragged me along through the crowd and over to a side door and out into the parking lot to a row of RVs.

"Go in there." She pointed at the second trailer in the lineup. "The makeup person is waiting for you."

"I don't need makeup. I'm just here to consult and most specialists don't bother with it," I protested. "They want me to look authentic, right?"

Valerie laughed, as if I had made a huge joke, patting me on the back. "Nothing in the movies is real, Professor. It's got to be bigger, better and far more exciting that real life to have an impact on an audience. You'll soon catch on. I've written you into a number of scenes. Let's hope you're photogenic."

Surprised, I still did what she asked of me without quarrel, walking up the three stairs and rapping on the metal door. Maybe the person working on me could teach me a few things?

"Come in, darlin'," a voice called out.

I opened the door and was greeted by a man and a woman sitting on two swivel chairs in front of a set of vanity mirrors.

"Oh, who do we have here?" the man said with a low whistle, his bright peacock smock standing out against his bright red hair and snow-white skin. His eyebrows were plucked into a thin line and his makeup was impeccable. "Come to Daddy!"

I smiled at his antics as he gestured at me. "Apparently, I need makeup."

"What? A woman as beautiful—*so* not necessary, darlin'. But humor me. I want to see if I can improve on nature, make you even more lovely to look at. Sit."

"You're in good hands, hon. Skye will make you look amazing on camera," the woman said. She smiled at me. "I'm Dawn, by the way."

We shook hands all round, then I plunked down where Skye suggested.

"Have you studied your lines yet? I can practice them with you if you want," Dawn said.

"Please! I just got handed the script and I have no idea what I'm doing." I might as well throw myself on the mercy of the court. They seemed like such friendly, helpful people.

"We'll have you fixed up and ready to act like a pro in no time," the pair said in unison, making all three of us laugh. Mine might have been a tad nervous sounding, but there wasn't a person alive who wouldn't be nervous to stand in front of a camera for the first time. Honestly, I was quaking in my boots, as the saying went.

"Close your eyes. I want it to be a surprise," Skye said, taking up a tube of something from the counter and turning to me expectantly. Our eyes met in the mirror, and I relaxed.

I sat and meditated for the few minutes it took.

"Ooh-la-la," he said. "You can open those gorgeous peepers now, darlin'."

I stared at myself. He'd done a brilliant job, making my eyes pop and my skin look like porcelain.

"Easy-peasy on someone who looks like you. Okay, now Dawn will help you with your lines. Then you can change into wardrobe." Skye moved away, poured himself a cup of coffee then sat down nearby to watch.

"I've marked what you're supposed to say in yellow highlighter. See," Dawn said, pointing at the script. "Fortunately, there's only a few today. But tonight, you got a bit more to study for, girlfriend."

I took the pages from Dawn and she began to read aloud from another copy she picked up off the counter. Nodding at me, she prompted me to read when it was my turn.

I took a deep breath and launched into it. "Nice to meet y'all." *What was I, a Southern Belle?* I continued, "But I need to talk to you alone, Johnny."

"'Excuse me, but duty calls.' Then you walk off together and Johnny says, 'What is it?'" Dawn said, her finger tracking across the page as she read. "You don't like your room?"

"I would prefer we sleep on different floors, if not different hotels. You know I'm with Mac now."

"Can't handle the temptation, sweetheart?"

"I can handle it just fine. I'm here to work—nothing else. Otherwise, get yourself another expert. I'm not here to play games of chance with you. I'll leave that to the risk-takers. I want a life built on mutual respect. Two people who share the same vision. Not with a man who only thinks of himself." I looked up from the script. "What's this? It sounds like I'm the love interest?"

"Hmm, did you not know? Logan gave the main character's ex-wife part to you. Now you have two reasons to be in the movie. But don't worry, there's no hanky-panky, darlin'. But isn't it exciting! You get to act in way more scenes!" Skye winked at me, as if I were the sly one.

My stomach dropped. "But I'll need to learn more lines on the fly."

"*Phttt*, happens all the time. Lines change on whim or with the weather. But you'll need a union card. No worries—I'm certain everything's being taken care of as we speak."

I stood up, antsy and royally pissed. "This was supposed to be an easy gig. I'm no actress. I'm a university professor, for heaven's sake!"

"But you look perfect for the role. Just watch out for jealousy on set."

"This is unacceptable. I won't take another's job away." I could only imagine how my taking over a lead role might annoy others. And at the last moment too.

"You didn't." Skye's face broke out into a huge grin. "But bless your heart for being a caring human being. I should have said upfront that the part is brand spanking new, combining your specialist role with uni-prof. But I think it adds to the film. I love me a bit of romance, even if it's biting repartee between two fighting exes."

I took a deep breath to find my center. What on earth had happened to my calm, well-ordered life? How had I ended up in the wrong man's bed—well if I wanted a man guaranteed to stick with me after the passion subsided, I would have chosen someone tame like Brad—and now had somehow become a bona-fide actress in the movie in the space of a single weekend?

"You are going to knock them dead, darlin'. Keep your chin up and watch your back. That's all there is to it." Skye put his hand over his heart. "You're a natural. What I wouldn't give for hair and skin like yours."

I managed a smile in return. Skye had a way of making me feel much better.

The door to the RV opened and Valerie poked her head in. "All set? We need you now, Professor."

"Best we get at it then." I pushed down my misgivings and braced myself, prepared to follow Valerie back into the ballroom.

Skye punched the air above him like Rocky celebrating a victory in the boxing ring. "Go get 'em, darlin'."

I snorted. I was about as far from *that* as I could be. I was comfortable in front of a class, but what about in front of professional actors when I wasn't one? I was good at improvising in the classroom, but saying the exact words I was given? *Please, please, let me remember my lines.*

Chapter Fifteen

Logan

"Places, everyone. Ten seconds," I said. I peered through the viewfinder, observing the dinner table scene while crouched over the camera operator's shoulder to double check for accuracy. An awkward position, but necessary. It looked good. Connor, an expert in all things film, had showcased the actors seated at the table perfectly. I gestured at the camera assistant to do his thing.

"Action!" I shouted a few seconds later. I loved that word. It held such promise, even if some directors had given up saying it. I still appreciated the old lingo more than the new. Terms that had been used for decades resonated with me. Like the use of an Abby Singer, the second-to-last shot of the day. It still had its place to revive a tired crew. But we were a long way from that at the moment with a full day of shooting ahead.

The digital image went live at that split second. I watched intently as Connor panned over the seven actors sitting at the table who all studiously avoided looking at the camera. Their job was to pretend they were not being filmed, but engrossed in watching and listening to the singer on stage.

"And *cut!*" I looked around. "Now, where's the professor?" I had decided it was best to keep things between Justine and myself professional, at least on set. I didn't want rumors abounding of my being distracted by her being there. Or any hint of nepotism. If they were to discover she's my very own Forever Mate, the charges would no doubt prove true.

"Here I am," Justine spoke up, coming into view along with my head writer, Valerie.

My mouth just about dropped open at how beautiful she looked. Untouchable. Like a shining star fallen to Earth. Did others see what I did? That she looked too fine for this world? All thoughts of being able to keep this perfectly professional dropped to the wayside, buried under the reality of how much seeing her affected my ability to think straight or hold another single thought in my head.

Connor stirred, giving a slight gasp at my side as my angel came on set and into his viewfinder. The simpleness of the blue dress that wardrobe had chosen only set her off more, her beauty not needing to compete with too much fuzziness. Maybe this was a bad idea? If the world was introduced to her, she'd be in demand in no time. What the hell had I been thinking? She should be kept away from the coarseness of the world. A smart wolf would squire her away to his castle and never let another lay eyes on her as long as they both shall live.

"Where did you find *her*?" Connor asked, not taking his eyes off the image before him for a second.

I said nothing, watching the other crew members take a far too close a look at the newest addition to our team. I didn't like the way some of the male actors perked up, licking their damn chops. So much for trying to keep this professional and avoiding jealousy issues. I needed to claim my angel before anyone else thought they had even the slightest chance of being with her. She was mine and mine alone.

"Aw, I see my intended has arrived. Everyone, I'm pleased to say that this is Professor Justine Bell, our newest actor to join the Creig Team."

Shocked faces turned my way and I just smiled the smile of the smug. My wolf preened, pleased that events had taken their proper course.

"Intended!" Connor echoed my word. This time he turned to stare me in the face. "When did this happen?"

"Recently."

"Doesn't she want anyone to know about it?" he asked, pointing at Justine. She looked stunned, like someone had leveled an unwarranted accusation at her. But I also saw her pull herself together a moment later. *Good.* She understood perfectly why I had said what I did.

"You know women, right? Well, Justine is even more private than most about her personal life." I needed to keep this going and not give anyone time to overthink things. I jumped into explaining the motivation for the scene.

"Okay, Justine, I want you to come up to the table and give Turner a look that tells the world that you have plenty of baggage between you. You're angry at him but won't give him the satisfaction of saying anything about it around his friends." I turned to her co-star to add, "Then you get up from the table, Turner, and move off to the side where your conversation with Justine takes place in private. Stand on the X on the floor. Got it?"

Turner nodded. Justine gave me a steely look, and I deemed her ready as well.

"Just like that, Justine. You got the right motivation," I said to cover up things.

"Action!"

Justine moved to the table, her body graceful yet restrained like it was a conversation she didn't want to have with Turner. *Good.* She looked amazing on camera. Her beef with me would only work to our advantage…which was how I would explain the ruse later.

I followed the action through the viewer as Justine gave Turner the look she had given me. Of course, there would be hell to pay. *No problem. I get what I want, one way or the other.* And my claiming her would keep her from any hassle from the male crew members. She could thank me later for that stroke of genius and foresight.

The pair exchanged terse words and when I yelled cut, a round of applause broke out for Justine's having done her first scene on set. *Nice.* She'd done an excellent job playing the ex of the lead. *Very believable.* She seethed with emotion, all caught forever on film.

But then she marched right over to me, her expression grim as she looked up at Connor and me on the dolly. "I want to talk to you. Now!"

"We need to set up for the next scene, so go right ahead, Logan," Connor said with a twist of his lips. "See to your *intended.*"

I jumped down from the dolly and gave her a smooch right there in front of the crew. Her body was stiff in my arms, but I ignored that and pulled her in tight for a huge hug.

"You were amazing. Well done, angel." Her body relaxed a bit and I patted her back. "Just go along with things. I have my reasons and they are sound," I whispered in her ear. Her womanly scent flooded my system and I was hard pressed to let her go. Problem was, another body part was overreacting to her presence, so it was best to back off for now. Later, I would have her all to myself. And what I had planned promised to keep her mind off questioning me and right onto what we both wanted. *Another night of incredible mind-blowing sex.*

"Do you have a free moment? There's something I want to show you in the prop room," she said, a gleam in her eyes.

I arched my brow at her. "Can't wait till tonight, angel?" I teased.

She just gave me a level look and turned to leave. "Coming?"

"Take ten everyone!" I yelled, though what I really wanted was hours to be alone with her. I took her arm and we left together. This day was looking better and better.

But when I closed the door behind us in the prop room, Justine didn't immediately jump my bones but turned to confront me.

"What were you thinking! I am *not* your intended! Don't you ever ambush me like that again!" She was so beautiful in that moment, her face flushed with color like we were making love already, her eyes sparkling like blue gems.

Oh yes you are. You are mine whether you know it yet or not. "I was thinking to keep other men away from you. Did you see the way they were practically drooling? I can't have that kind of upset on my shoot. I needed to take action, keep you protected. Plus, it did give you the proper motivation for the scene. You played it perfectly." I smiled, hoping my dimples were popping. They seem to charm the ladies. At least they had in the past.

"I don't need protection. I can damn well stand up for myself. You had no right saying such a thing. And why in the hell would you do that anyway? We're just hanging around together, having fun. We just met. And we certainly have not made a commitment to not see other people." She still looked angry, shaking her head, her lips tightly pressed together.

"Are you seeing anyone else?" Jealousy struck like a thunderbolt. What the hell was going on here? *Is she not feeling what I am? Two stars colliding and becoming one. That destiny has chosen us.* I pressed a hand to my chest, dimly aware of sharp pain following her words. And here I had been thinking that if I changed, gave up my playboy ways and quit putting myself out there, that the woman meant for me would fall into my arms and we'd be together from then on.

Fate had been cruel if my fated mate was not ready to be with me or didn't want to be with me permanently. Was this my angel rejecting me? My brain stuttered, denying the idea with extreme prejudice. No, it couldn't be anything but a small misunderstanding. I needed to discuss this further with my brothers—they seemed to understand having so recently been through the process. *Keep your eye on the prize, reel her in slowly and keep up the pressure* had been their combined advice. But I needed specifics, not vague pronouncements.

She must have seen something in my posture or expression, because the anger appeared to drain out of her.

"I'm not ready to talk about such things yet, Logan. We just met. I'm a scholar. I don't believe in love at first sight. I believe it takes time to build a relationship. It's easy to be what the other person needs at first, but it's often faked to create a sense of two people being compatible. I need time. I need to see you as you really are before I would ever consider us being exclusive. Besides, you'll be quitting Vegas after the shoot. And where does that leave us?"

"Have you been playing me false? Are you not who you say you are?" The words hurt like hell to say, but I needed to know. *Is my angel real?*

"I'm sorry. I didn't explain that very well. Yes, I am who I say I am. It's just too soon, all right? We hardly know each other. But you should know that I'm not looking for anything permanent." She gestured between the two of us with a graceful hand movement. "Yes, the sex is fantastic—best I've ever had or imagined it could be. But there's far more to life than setting the sheets on fire. There's being there through the hard times when men—people," she said, correcting herself, "find it easier to go out and have a fling instead of doing the hard thing of working through their differences. My dad may have loved my mother, but his head was easily turned by a beguiling smile and my mom paid a terrible price for his lack of moral fiber. It broke her heart."

I processed what she was trying to say over the pain of her rejection. Maybe it was clearer cut than I'd thought — she just needed reassurance that I was never going back to being a playboy. "Okay, I understand your father ran around on your mother. Not all men do that. I would *never* step out on my woman. When a Creig commits, it's for life. You have my word on that."

"Why are we having this conversation now? Not like you could possibly be ready to commit to me."

Now she looked uncomfortable, not meeting my eye. I wanted to talk more about this, but something stopped me from pressing it harder. I would have to show her that I had changed. That I would never break her heart once she honored me with giving hers over to my care. This was new for me., new and acutely uncomfortable. I had always pushed hard for what I wanted and never made any bones about saying so, but she was a prize worth waiting for. I just hoped she wouldn't break my heart any more than she already had. Another hit like this one and I wasn't certain of the outcome. So, a compromise was in order.

"When the shoot is finished, you can make all the announcements you like about our relationship status. That work for you?"

"Maybe. I don't know. But I didn't see any drooling going on out there." She pointed through the wall to Nero's where the film crew was waiting. "I think you overreacted, Logan Creig. Just so you know, I'm no one's *intended*." She let out a whoosh of breath, like she was glad it was all settled. It was not, but I would have to bide my time, and man up.

"Okay, I'll let it pass if it keeps things quieter on set. But there's something else I want to share with you if you have a moment?" she said.

The abrupt change of subject was noted.

"For you, I have all the time in the world." Still unsettled by our discussion, though encouraged I knew more about her than before, I said the words automatically. God, this was a minefield of my own making. If only I had a stellar reputation, none of this would have happened. But then, my brothers weren't exactly saints and they'd landed in their happy places.

"Hardly!" She laughed a bit awkwardly but like she was really trying to smooth things over, taking the sting out of her words. "You have a movie to get in the can. That's how they say it, right?"

"What do you want to show me?" I asked, intrigued in spite of things.

She led the way to a table with the artifact that I had had delivered to the university only this morning.

"What's this doing back? I thought you wanted to run tests?"

"We did. Come, press your hand here."

Her voice was tinged by even more excitement than earlier. Damn it all to hell, but she seemed more intrigued with the artifact than with the idea of a relationship. But I did as she asked. The sooner this was over, the quicker we could get to sneaking in some pleasure time. I wanted to be with her. It was the only thing that could bring us closer after what was said. Only sex could renew our bond after a disagreement. According to my brothers, the best part of arguing was making up afterwards.

"Here?" I asked, more interested in looking at her then where my hand was going.

"Yes, right there."

Nothing happened.

"What?" she asked, her expression disappointed and confused. "Huh. Let me show you."

She replaced my hand with hers. The device began to glow before it cracked open a few centimeters and light escaped, transforming into a swirling hologram. A bright star shape appeared, hovering above the table.

Stunned, I could only stare at it.

"Speak English," she said in a commanding tone.

"*A member of the Homo sapiens, humankind, of which there are forty-nine million, one hundred and seventeen thousand and thirty-three on planet Earth. Amenemope, son of Psusennes I, reigns in Egypt at present date, 1001 BC.*"

The star suddenly stopped talking, the light dimmed and everything retracted back inside the object, like it had never happened.

"What the hell? Was that some kind of recording?"

"I don't know why it didn't work for you. It should have," she said, a frown creasing the smooth skin of her forehead between those gorgeous eyes.

"Try it again," she insisted, taking my hand and laying it over the same spot hers had just been.

Nothing happened. She shook her head, pursing her lips. "Why doesn't it work for you?"

I ran my hands over the device, noting so many symbols, no two alike. I pressed against a few, but nothing opened the egg.

"I wonder how this thing came to be?"

"Professor Dixon at the university examined it and the tests reveal it's not made of any substance known to be of earthly origin."

I continued working my way around the egg, systematically pressing each slight indentation. Then it happened. The egg came to life again. The bright star spoke once more. "*Man-wolf of the species Lycan, sub-species Wulver, of which there are one thousand and forty-*"

nine on planet Earth. Amenemope, son of Psusennes I, reigns in Egypt at present date, 1001 BC."

Holy fuck. I suddenly understood what was going on. This was an interstellar or extraterrestrial object from another location in the universe, created during the twenty-first dynasty. Fixated at the very idea, my mind raced with what this could mean to all species now forced to hide on Earth to protect themselves from predatory humans. Would it be our salvation? Or our doom? The ramifications too huge for a single moment in time, I turned to look at my angel.

She had stopped moving or breathing at my side. A shimmering feeling overcame me, my body wanting to shift. I held on with determination, not wanting to expose anything more about who I was. Or what I was. That hurdle was too far to even think about today. Just another thing that could drive us apart.

Gathering myself, I finally asked, touching her cheek gently, "Are you okay?"

Her eyes wide, so wide the white showed around the intense blue of her irises, she shook her head, locking glances with me.

"You"—she pointed at me with an accusatory finger—"you're not fully human, according to this thing. Is this some kind of trick you're pulling on me?"

My heart muscle clenched, bruised by the accusation.

"No trick. And I'm still the same man," I said. "This proves nothing. It's a child's game." My scathing tone changed the dynamics in the room and cleared my head. I had to make this thing disappear. This was a huge development. One that would send a tsunami shock through the supernatural world. What was it The Creig always said, *only love can give us the ability to accept*

147

what is different from ourselves. Pure love, one that loved unconditionally, did not exist for others seen as different on Earth as yet. Maybe it never would, but in the meantime, I needed to get rid of the evidence ASAP.

She blinked then, trying to absorb things. Her thoughts were obviously not in order at the moment. "Did you set this up? As some kind of joke on the new consultant? No, that doesn't make any sense! The substance it's made of – it's not of earthly origin, which proves it's far more than that. No way this is fake. What's going on, Logan?"

I shrugged. Her accusation still stung. "I had nothing to do with it showing up here. I have no idea at all what it's doing here. It's not my hoax. I would never want to trick you."

But guilt hit, hard, knowing I was hiding something from her. Something that could blow up in my face. I wasn't fully human. A double-edged sword hung over my head, knowing humans weren't ready for me – for anything different. They only saw our kind through the eyes of the 'other', not as we were. Flawed, but in all the ways that count, family, friends and community, just as human as they were.

"I want to know more." She let out a deep breath. "About the man I'm spending time with. I'm sorry I said those horrible words about not being human, and there's no reason for you to want to trick me. I wish I could take them back. Please, accept my apology."

"Apology accepted." The words about not wanting a real relationship hurt far more.

"I'm still confused about this thing," she said, interrupting my dark thoughts as she pointed at the artifact. "It seems not always to be right. Obviously, you're not a werewolf!" Her laugh was shaky. "But there are symbols for many of the creatures thought to be legends. Do you think maybe some of them could be real? Is this a message sent from space? Or maybe just a historical record of mythology and only humans actually exist?"

"I have no idea. I'm as much in the dark as you are. But it will be looked into, you have my word." I had come into the room wanting nothing more than a few minutes alone with her, and now time was getting away from me. Not to mention I needed to report this ticking bomb to my fellow weres as soon as possible.

But first I had something important to do. I pulled her close, hugging her to my heart, needing to heal it by pressing my flesh to hers. Once I felt her naked against me, all would be well.

We kissed and the world dropped away. It was just us again, two hearts beating as one, and the delicious passion we shared overtaking everything else in the universe. It made sense of the world, at least for me. *But you can't always be making love with this woman. It takes far more than that to create a love connection.* I pushed the unwanted thoughts aside with extreme force and focused on the moment.

Chapter Sixteen

Justine

"We should head back. You said ten minutes. It's gone well past that." I pulled up my underwear and smoothed the blue dress. I liked the wardrobe chosen for my character in the movie, simple lines and classic styling that I would have bought for myself given the chance. But damn, what was I thinking? I couldn't be around Logan for five minutes without wanting to jump into bed together. Though this was more a stand-up session. *My, but he has strong, uplifting arms.*

"They can't start without me. And everyone's used to the *hurry up and wait* scenario on set. They still get paid and if a shoot takes longer, just more cash in their pockets." He straightened his clothes, his hair falling over his forehead making him look so much more approachable. And younger. I reached up and pushed the thick locks back into place with my hands.

"I don't think I would enjoy that being the case. I need to control my day more."

"I appreciate the honesty." Logan shrugged, his eyes hooded, his expression unreadable. "But it's not all that bad. Actors text, read, play games, socialize, even knit while they're waiting for their cue."

"I wouldn't want the life. This is the only acting gig I'm going to be involved in. Ever. Then it's right back to teaching and writing books or papers." My mind again drifted to the artifact sitting like the proverbial elephant in the room. *What the hell is its story?* My curiosity was aroused to the point that I wanted to jump right into doing research. Maybe starting with the bill of lading as to where it came from exactly? If it wasn't for my needing to stay in Vegas for the shoot, I would be flying to Egypt to talk to anyone who knew anything about it.

"Have you ever considered how you would make a relationship work if the person has to travel a lot for their career?" Logan gave me an intense look, as if my answer had a lot riding on it.

"Not really. Though I'm of a mind if two people are meant to be together, they'll make it work somehow. Not many places in the world are inaccessible these days."

I moved toward the Infinity Egg, feeling its pull. Or maybe to avoid the way the conversation was going again. I was not looking to be with any man permanently at the moment, no matter how much I enjoyed being with him. Something he darn well knew now. It would only spell trouble when his eye was drawn to another, as much as he swore it would never happen. In my experience a leopard *never* changed his spots, just used charming smiles to hide them.

The thought hurt like hell, imagining Logan being with another woman, but better knowing now than being broadsided later. Love was the direct route to pain and I'd rather be alone than take that chance. Not that I wanted to become the lady with ten cats, but surely there were other ways to fill the void in my heart? My relationship with Marnie and a couple of other women helped. Sure, going home to a cold bed at night sucked. But that was the cost to keep oneself protected.

I ran my hand over the other images carved on the sarcophagus, composing myself and wishing I could set off another bit of intel like Logan had done. Guilt hit that I had said such a terrible thing about not being human to a man who had only wanted to spend time with me. I needed to make that up to him. But darn it, he had to know that saying I was his intended was a terrible decision and would make things only more awkward going forward.

At least I had straightened it out, made myself clear. It was what I wanted, right? Shut down all thoughts of this going any further before someone gets hurt. Because someone always gets hurt, no matter how much they say it won't happen.

I forced my mind onto other things now, not liking the pain I felt at my actions, and at this thing, whatever it was between him and I, being over. I stared at the artifact. It would be cool to hear how much the messages varied. Maybe that would be the ticket? The DNA code of another person could cause a different message to appear each time. One per visitor. I wanted to test that immediately, bring in people off the street to check out the theory.

"Will you have the artifacts ready to be set in their cases for tomorrow night's shoot?" Logan asked.

"I'm done filming for today, right?"

He nodded. "Until tomorrow afternoon."

"Then I can get right to it. I should be able to wrap things up in a few hours."

"How about dinner tonight? I should finish filming by eight o'clock or so. Dinner and a movie night might be fun."

He sounded so formal. Like he'd taken a step backward. I couldn't blame him considering how I had approached his wanting to make more of what was going on between us than actually was. But it didn't feel near as good as I had hoped. Damn, but life was complicated. This was why I avoided any talk of commitment like the plague. I knew my own mind so well. Okay, maybe it made me sound selfish, but I had a tender heart that needed to be protected at all costs. But I wanted the old Logan back. The fun, bantering one who kept the world at bay.

"Add in some hot, buttery popcorn and I'm all yours."

"So, it only takes the mention of a treat to get you onboard." He smiled that sexy one that made his dimples pop and my heart somersaulted, damn it.

"I'm easy, sir, what can I say?" And just like that we were back.

"In that case, I'll hire a world-class chef and have him make all your wished-for treats. What's your favorite decadent food?"

"Anything with whipped cream. What's your dessert of choice?" I licked my lips, forgetting everything else, enjoying how his eyes flared to a brilliant green. I knew he was remembering feeding me from his own hands. The innocence of that moment held me spellbound.

"Chocolate, whipped cream and strawberries. Preferably enjoyed in bed."

"Then I guess we have a date for later." I liked being on a better footing with Logan, more than I cared to admit.

"Guess we do."

The door closed behind him a second later.

Time to get to work. I gave a loud sigh, looking around the space. I wanted to investigate the Infinity Egg, but I had other tasks that needed doing first. All the artifacts needed to be prepped and loaded into their special containers ready to be rolled out into the main hotel convention center. The pretend heist, the robbery of the golden Egyptian recreations, would take place tomorrow night and for the rest of the week. It was a major part of the movie plot.

But first I needed to change my clothes and get into something easier to work in. I grabbed my backpack and slipped out of the prop room, headed for the ladies' bathroom. I had been given exclusive access to a private section inside and I intended to enjoy the privilege.

A sense of unease crept over me as I observed the gangster guy once again standing in the hallway. The John Gotti look-alike was busy texting on his phone, but he glanced up at me for an uncomfortable second, sending a streak of unease straight through me from the cold deadliness of his eyes that was right back in place. Then recognition of having met me earlier seemed to hit though and his expression shifted, softened. He gave me a curt nod. Annoyed by the sensation of discomfort his presence brought on, I shook it off, nodded back at him and hurried to push through the door marked *women*.

I had a quick rinse off in the private space complete with sink, shower stall and mirror. *Gotta love the luxury of the Glitter Palace!* Then changed into jeans, a stretchy top and running shoes. Pulling my hair up into a bunch with my hands, I slipped a scrunchie into place to make a high pony, enjoying the sensation of my neck being unencumbered. Tucking the set clothes into my backpack, I made note of needing to return them to wardrobe later.

I pulled out my phone and called up Marnie's number, needing some perspective on the Logan situation.

"Hey, me matey. What's up?" she asked.

"Just did my first lines on set and we did it in one take," I said, unable to keep from bragging.

"Well done, you."

"But, the thing is, Logan called me his *intended*."

"Whoa. Bit soon for that, don't you think?"

"Exactly. I called him out on it. Let him know flat-out that I have no intention of marrying anyone — ever."

"Really?" She gave a low whistle. "How'd he take it?"

"Surprised, I think. I guess no woman has turned him down before."

"Probably not. I mean, take one look at the guy and you know that. So, you're not going to see each other again? Other than for work, of course."

"Well, no, we're having a dinner and a movie night."

"So you *do* like him? Miss Commitment-phobe?"

"What? Just because I care about protecting myself doesn't mean if the right guy came along, and we're a perfect match, both understanding that passion is no substitute for the hard work of staying together, that it has little place in the real world of building a family, that I wouldn't consider a mutual agreement."

"Can you hear yourself, girlfriend? Really, loving someone is not all cut and dried. There's give and take. Sure, you hardly know this Logan. But by the sound of it, you're not even willing to give it a chance *just because* you're drawn so irresistibly to him. That makes no sense. Passion is messy, sure, but it can be the foundation of a real life together. It's a start. You gotta give it a chance. There's no other way unless you want to end up with someone like Brad, or worse yet, a cat lady."

That cut to the bone. "I'm allergic to cats."

She laughed out loud over the phone. "Are you allergic to Logan?"

She had me there.

"I gotta go. Talk soon?"

"You bet." I ended the call. Time to get to work. I just hoped that gangster guy was gone by now. But luck was not with me today. When I stepped out of the bathroom, there he stood, staring at his phone, not three meters away.

Should I stay? Head for Nero's? Right now, seeing Logan walk down the hallway toward me would be the sweetest sight in all the world. I had no doubt his mere presence would chase off this man. *Crap.* Was this guy interested in the prop room? Casing the joint? Or just an innocent bystander waiting for someone to arrive like before? I didn't know his patterns, only having just started this job. For all I knew, he showed up every day to meet a friend.

I had the key card in my hand, but I hesitated, unsure of the best course of action. Every instinct screamed to be careful.

Deciding to just grow a pair as I had important work to do, I hurried to get inside the room, breathing a bit better when the door closed behind me. Maybe it was all in my imagination? He had talked politely with that strange guy from that witness group earlier who hadn't taken my rejection of his invite at all well. Maybe the guy just needed some Botox to loosen up that deep frown.

I stepped on something that made my foot slip, drawing my attention downward. A thin white envelope lay on the floor, pushed under the door while I'd been cleaning up because I was certain it hadn't been there earlier. I tore open the flap and withdrew the single sheet of white paper. It was covered in pieces cut and glued from newspapers and magazines like a puzzle. Words. The message was short and to the point. My breathing tightened as I read the message.

WE DEMAND THE ARTIFACTS. LEAVE THE DOOR UNLOCKED AND WALK AWAY, PROFESSOR. TELL NO ONE. WE ARE WATCHING.

Chills raced up and down my spine while sweat dampened my armpits. Someone had been spying on me. Did this have something to do with that group, Creation's Witnesses, from earlier? Or the man in black hanging around the prop room?

I needed to figure this out. My first instinct was to run straight to Logan, but he would take it the wrong way and go too far with it. Not to mention he was busy—there was nothing I hated more than being interrupted by Dean Two-Times while I lectured. But hell, Logan couldn't even handle men looking at me askance. I shook my head. No, I didn't want to be on lockdown. But I needed to feel safe to do my job.

Hmm. There was an implied threat, though not spelled out in actual words like *we're going to hurt you*. I shuddered at that idea. No, best guess, opportunists wanting an easy score. Well, not on my shift. What I needed was a security guard to have my back, a bodyguard. And this complex was filled with them. This could be solved easily enough without running to Logan.

It hit me then that this was the perfect excuse *not* to be involved with the movie going forward. And just as fast the realization slapped me that I wanted to stay onboard. The Infinity Egg intrigued me like no artifact ever before. I trampled down the other thought that I wanted this time with Logan a great deal as well. No, a few weeks of passion was all it was, all it could be. But I wanted *that* at least. If I allowed this information out, things might spiral right out of my control. Decision made, I carefully checked the hallway, found it deserted — thank heavens — locked the prop room door and scurried down the corridor toward a door marked *security* that I'd observed earlier.

But when I arrived, I found the office deserted. Apparently, everyone was out and about doing their jobs. *Great.* But of course that was what they should be doing. Drumming my fingers on the counter, I considered my options. Did I wait? Call it a day? Oh, but the Infinity Egg needed my immediate attention. And Logan and I had a date for later. Thoughts of a few wonderful hours of research while Logan was busy directing fired up my brain. Okay, I'd just leave a note for security to contact me. I scribbled my information on a pad of paper and left the single sheet draped over a keyboard where it was certain to be noticed.

Reminding myself to stay extra vigilant, I kept a sharp eye out, but nothing appeared amiss on the trek back to the prop room. Good grief, but the Glitter Palace was a huge complex, even by Vegas standard. Finally, I was back inside sanctuary. Now for some special time. *But, Justine, you'd better finish the work you promised to do for the movie.* I dutifully set about placing the golden treasurers into their special housings, making quick work of it with the egg calling me every little while. *There.* All done. Now on to bigger and better things.

I began checking the symbols on the artifact against known pictographs online at a website reserved for other like-minded scholars and unavailable to the general public.

Then, a terrible shrieking overpowered all my senses, rudely waking me from my trance. It pierced my brain. The damn fire alarm had gone off. It sent all my senses reeling. Damn it! Just when I was making such great headway.

Chapter Seventeen

Justine

I peeled off my gloves with annoyance and threw them in the bin. Of all times for a fire alarm. The Infinity Egg had gotten right under my skin and each second with it was riveting, essential. I might be the first person to investigate the object in thousands of years. The weight of the importance of doing my work well at this moment in history could not be overstressed. I was breaking new territory, and a brand-new day awaited if it proved to be the real deal. And nothing so far had dissuaded me of that final outcome. Everything checked out.

The banshee screaming in my ears seemed to have increased and I cringed at the annoying continuous wall of sound. I had to leave, but abandoning the egg to a fire seemed wrong. Surely any flame would be contained quickly, right? I dithered, hoping the alarm would stop, meaning it was a false one.

No dice.

I had to leave before someone charged in and demanded it, making me look foolish. Not to mention that damn noise was giving me a splitting headache.

I couldn't carry the artifact—though light, it was far too large and awkward for one person to handle, so I had to pray that it would remain safe. Maybe I could have a word with a fireman and ask them to protect this room? Explain the value of the artifacts it contained? That at least would be something I could do.

No more time.

I hurried to the door and opened it. But before I could step all the way outside, a large body was in my way, slamming me backward. *What the hell?*

Something hard pressed tight against my ribs, bruising them in the process, making me gasp as the door closed again with terrible finality, locking me and the intruder inside.

"Don't say a word or I'll shoot you," he barked loudly over the oppressive noise, pressing a hand over my mouth. His tone was guttural, close to my ear. I could smell the unpleasant odors of garlic and onions. "Can you hear me?"

I nodded, my bladder about to let loose. I fought to hold on to it and he half held me up, my nerves shattering under the pressure. I got a good look at him, recognizing the mafia guy from earlier.

"You scream, I shoot. Understand?"

Who would hear me anyway? He had to shout in my ear for me to hear him.

He took his hand away. I had no doubt the man meant business. My life was hanging by a thread and the complex was emptying of people who might help.

The alarm was still firing off, hurting my ears and making me want to flee.

"Start walking." He made a slight gesture with the deadly gun in his hand, pointing it right at me. "We're going all the way to the back. My brothers are waiting outside. Your key also opens that door. Convenient, isn't it?"

Was I supposed to agree? I stumbled along on shaky legs, my hands trembling as I led the way through the maze. My clothes were already half-soaked with sweat. I shivered, cold and fearful.

The outside entrance was a large steel door. *God, I hope my key card works.* Because if it didn't, I knew without a doubt I was toast.

My hands were shaking so badly that it took three tries to do the sequence correctly. Then the door flew open and two more large, intimidating men burst into the room. Both had hoodies over their heads. As soon as they were inside, they pushed the coverings back out of the way.

"Took you long enough," one man said, his voice filled with discontent. His bulldog face was highlighted by a shaved head. The other man was taller and slimmer, a Slim Jim, his hair as black as my capturers.

"We gotta work quickly. Someone may have seen something," the guy who'd accosted me warned.

"Didn't you take care of the surveillance camera?" Bulldog asked.

"Yeah, but who knows who's watching." The guy with the gun shrugged.

"Then what are we standing around for?" Slim Jim asked.

The four of us hurried forward. My feet nearly left the floor as they hustled me along.

"You, show us the gold," gun guy said, pointing at me.

I nodded and pointed. "All of the specially created artifacts are in those individually crafted boxes."

"Ah, the most special artifact of all," he said, stopping in front of the Infinity Egg.

"That's just a prop. It's not worth anything. Not made of gold or jewels or anything." What if they decided to take it and ruined it, trying to force it open? Though it appeared unbreakable, who knew for certain? For me, it was the most priceless item in the room.

"Right," the man said in a scoffing tone. "Good try, Professor, but we know what it is."

My heart sank at his statement. How had they known? Who were these men?

In short order, the two men filled their arms with the items, while fake John Gotti kept his gun pointed at me. It took them seven trips apiece, but they soon had all the rich artifacts moved out of the storeroom, including the egg. *God, please don't let them kill me.* I had seen their faces. *Would they let me live?*

"Okay, all done. What we gonna do about her?" Bulldog asked, raising a dark slash of eyebrow in my direction.

The fire alarm had finally ceased, making it easier to hear him though an intense ringing still obscured my hearing. Would someone come and check on me now? *Please let Logan or somebody wonder if I'm okay.*

"Boss wants her brought in as well."

"What? No, I won't tell anyone, I promise." I turned to run, my feet taking on a mind of their own as I moved toward the door. But I was grabbed before I could make it two steps.

I screamed. The guy bruised my ribs once more with the gun. "Shut it or you die right now. That what you want, Professor?"

I shook my head. Then I was pulled along toward the back entrance that led to the alley, my feet dragging. What was going to happen to me? My ordered life had fallen apart. *Wait.* He'd called me Professor. That meant they knew who I was…

Chapter Eighteen

Logan

I was so engrossed filming the scene of the lead being accosted by the man he owed money to that when a series of discordance sounds meant to halt everything in its tracks brought everyone else to their knees, I was more pissed than anything. The horrible eardrum-piercing sound had ruined the perfect shot.

"Damn it, now of all times!"

Everyone around me was realizing they had to exit the building. I didn't smell smoke, meaning it could be a false alarm and that thought made me even angrier.

"Gotta go, Logan," Connor said, shaking his head in dismay. His expression said it all. The perfect shot had been ruined, setting us back hours. Now my set people would need to replace the broken items destroyed by the actions of the lead and his antagonist when they had an altercation over the money owed and the woman they both loved. Not expensive, just time consuming and thereby annoying. And tomorrow, we were supposed to begin filming the actual heist, meaning I might need to rearrange things, which was always an annoyance to actors and production people alike.

Together we jumped down off the dolly and headed for the nearest exit. Outside in the glaring Vegas sun, I shielded my eyes with a pair of sunglasses and began moving between the various groups standing around the parking lot to check that everyone had made it out safely.

I kept an eye out for my angel, but as the seconds ticked by, I couldn't spot her anywhere. Where was she? I sent her a quick text as I continued looking. But as the minutes passed, I couldn't catch even a glimpse of her. *Damn it, where are you, Justine?*

Finally, the deafening sound halted.

"False alarm, folks, you can head back inside now." A friendly fireman spoke to us as he trudged back across the pavement, weighed down by all his heavy equipment. It was a hot day to be dressed like that and my sympathies were with him, even as my worry about Justine began to escalate. Something was wrong. All my instincts fired up and I ran toward the door, desperate to find her. To see her safe. She might not be willing to admit the extent of our connection yet, but the way my heart squeezed at thoughts of her missing said it all.

I opened the prop room door and hurried inside as it slammed shut behind me, my breath tight in my lungs.

"Justine!" I shouted, frantically looking around. The shelves and boxes were empty, bits of debris strewn around. What the hell! What had happened? I ran through the room toward the back, calling her name. But the room was empty.

Shit. The back door was propped open. Someone had robbed the place, meaning the fire alarm had been a diversion to hide their activities. I could smell the stink of others lingering in the air, a miasma of odors that sickened my stomach. *Oh my God.* Had they taken Justine with them?

Outside again, I looked both ways down the alley. A large white van was just exiting the far end. That had to be them! I had to track it—there was no other way. I had to shift. Nothing else for it.

No sooner had I thought of my wolf than I was out and running, shedding my clothes as I moved. Mid-stride, I entered another realm, a parallel existence, invisible from Earth, and my body underwent the change. On the other side, through the shimmering portal, the sensation deepened until all my cells had transformed, aligned in a new way. Then I was back in the present. Wolf. Instantly the world had mutated to an array of colors unknown to the human eye, blacks and browns and grays with subtle shadings that my brain converted to what my human side saw—blues and greens, yellow and reds. I breathed in deeply, my olfactory nerves sharpened by the transformation. The odor of the criminals filled my nostrils.

I raced toward the end of the alley the van had just vacated. I caught a glimpse of it turning onto the main road and increased my pace, my paws gaining purchase on the burning pavement. I ignored the shouts of people noticing a wolf running down the Vegas Strip.

I would be filmed, but I didn't give a shit. Only finding my angel mattered now. *If those bastards harm one hair on her head, they're all going to meet their doom.* I'd tear them limb from limb for taking my Forever Mate. Soon I would persuade her of that fact, then she would fall under my spell and never want to leave my side. She made me want to be a better man, the very reason people fell in love. I just had to make her see that.

My paws ate up the distance, my brain focused on keeping the van in plain view. The sounds of a car horn broke through my consciousness and I swerved to avoid a collision, loping between vehicles, trying to avoid being hit. I stayed away from the sidewalk, not wanting to hurt a human in my scramble to follow Justine.

One vehicle, a tour bus, suddenly veered too close. It struck my shoulder and I stumbled, barely able to keep my footing. Limping, I managed to keep up the chase. Nothing would stop me now short of death.

Thank God traffic eased as we reached the city limits. The van turned off the main road onto a side street, slowing.

I didn't slow down but continued the punishing pace, my heart muscle taxed to the limit from the massive amounts of blood flowing through it.

Up ahead, I could see a large compound. The van halted. A man leaned out of the driver's window and pressed a button to open the gate. I kept running and squeezed through the massive steel door just as it was closing. The mechanism caught my tail and sharp pain shot through me as a section of it ripped away. Ignoring it, I raced ahead, the sun bearing down on my body as if trying to press me into the roadway.

The vehicle stopped a hundred meters later in front of a large mansion with grilled windows and tight security. What was this place? I raced right up to the van, ignoring my own safety, and attacked the first man who jumped from the driver's seat. My vision had narrowed, my only thought protecting my angel. An ancient force had overtaken me. It did not reason the right or wrong of things, only of saving my mate. I grabbed the second man as he came out of the passenger door. Shouts erupted from the back of the vehicle as I reduced his threat to zero. He'd live, but right now he was incapacitated.

"What the hell!" A third man pulled Justine from the van and was staring at a wolf. Me. She stood by his side, her expression terrified. A gun appeared in the kidnapper's hand and he pointed it my way.

A shot rang out as I leaped for his throat. Sudden pain erupted in my side and I fell, taking him down with me.

I held on to the man, shaking him like a rag doll. Then he was still. Justine hadn't moved. Stunned, she stood frozen, staring at the carnage. Her hands were bound.

We had to get out of there. I had to shift. Drive us back to the casino. Protecting her might cause me to lose her, but I'd do it again in a heartbeat.

I pushed myself to enter the portal, the pain of my injuries making it that much more difficult. They would heal, most likely, like the men I'd dealt with, not knowing how badly I was injured. I was a bloody mess. No help for that.

Finally, I became human, having forced the change. I stumbled and fell to the ground at Justine's feet, the pain overtaking me as the world tilted.

"Logan," she whispered, her eyes wide with terror as she knelt at my side.

"We have to go. Others will come," I said through gritted teeth. "Help me up."

She did and I managed to regain my footing. We shambled along to the front of the van and I caught sight of men streaming out the front door of the mansion.

"Hurry! No time to lose."

She helped me inside the vehicle then followed right behind me. She pushed me over to the passenger side and sat in the driver's seat. The van leaped to life as she gunned the motor. She made a tight U-turn on the pavement before heading us down the road that led back to Vegas. Shouts and gunshots erupted behind us. The back window took a hit and blew out, sending shards of glass into the van. They didn't reach us and I was grateful that Justine wasn't cut.

My wounds were bleeding profusely. I pressed my hand to my side.

"I need something to staunch the blood." I took a quick look around. Nothing.

She tore off her top, loosening her hold on the steering wheel and causing us to fishtail down the road.

"Here." She straightened the wheel, and looking like a ghost she was so pale, managed to keep driving us in the right direction.

"Are they following?" I asked, wincing from the pain as I pressed the fabric against the bullet hole. It appeared the bullet had gone straight through me. I had another wound on my lower back from the altercation with the gate, but it was less serious.

"No." Her lips were tense as the small word escaped. Thank God she wasn't asking the hard questions. *Yet.*

Chapter Nineteen

Justine

"Do you have lupophobia as well as arachnophobia?" Logan asked, pressing my shirt to his wound, a crooked smile on his face.

"What?" *Am I hallucinating? Maybe I'm drugged?* Had Logan really been a wolf and taken down three men? None of this felt real. I had to be in some kind of dreamlike state that accounted for what I had just seen. A nightmare. *Get a hold of yourself, Bell. We have bigger problems. He's hurt, bleeding profusely. He needs a doctor.*

I looked over at him. Yes, he was still there, covered in blood. I'd do what I should, whether it was real or not. "We're going straight to the hospital."

"No need."

"Of course, there's a need! You've been shot, for heaven's sake!" That was, if I could believe my own eyes. Surreal wasn't a big enough word to explain what it felt like, sitting there driving after what I had just witnessed.

"I'll heal."

I glanced over at him again. "You're covered in blood, Logan. You need medical assistance." Why was he not more worried? This can't be real, then. *Please, let me wake up.* I pinched my arm hard. Harder.

"Ouch!"

"What's the matter? Are you hurt?" he demanded.

"No. You're the one bleeding. I just pinched myself because this doesn't make any sense at all." Then I thought of the Infinity Egg in the back of the van. It had said that Logan was a—what was the word? Yes, Wulver, a sub-species of Lycan. Could it be correct? If that was the case, then other supernatural creatures existed and— *No, don't go there.* My mind was reeling, like I was on the Tilt-A-Whirl at the fair. Nauseous now, I needed to pull over.

"I have to stop."

"What's wrong?"

I jerked the van to a halt and jumped out then leaned over and dry-heaved onto the side of the road. There was nothing to throw up as I had eaten so little of late. I stood there and stared at the Vegas skyline, feeling like nothing I had learned up until now was much compared to what was going on in the moment. What was being revealed threw my entire world into disorder. My whole thought process was in doubt and I was uncertain about getting my bearings back. *How is any of this possible?*

Then Logan was at my side, dressed in a pair of blue overalls he'd pulled out of the back of the van. How did he find something to wear? Then I remembered the artifacts had been covered with a tarp and some old clothes to protect them. At least dressed, he looked less intimidating and the clothes had the added advantage of hiding the copious amounts of blood.

"You shouldn't be walking around. You've been shot. You should rest."

"I'm already healing. I'll be fine."

"Because you're not human?" I asked, needing to hear him say it.

"I'm human. Think of it as more like a superpower. I can heal quicker than others, run faster, see in the dark. Definitely stronger for the DNA."

"And become a killing machine." My words were accusatory, but I couldn't help that. I was owed a proper explanation.

"They're not dead. But it's only because they were going to hurt you. Otherwise, you would not have known about any of this."

"You were going to hide something of this magnitude from me forever?"

"No, but we live by a code of honor to protect ourselves. You're not supposed to know what I am. It's dangerous to us. It's our number-one rule as a clan."

"I thought you called yourselves a pack?" My mind went back to the little I knew about werewolf mythology. *Correction – it's no myth.* Did that mean everything humans thought of as myth...was, well, real? My brain stuttered at the power of the impact. This was not going to be easy, getting my mind around this new world order.

"We call ourselves the Highland Heathens Clan. As to our history, Viking blood was added to our numbers during the invasions of Scotland in the eighth century. We're a powerful mix of the Viking wolf Fenrir that heralds the end of the world during the Ragnarök, and warrior blood, unbeatable on the battlefield."

"That's some legacy." I swallowed against the sensation of everything being out of control.

"A similar legacy exists for others related to us. Cristaldo, for instance, is connected to one of the three houses located in Vegas, House of Luceres, the others being Anche and Ribelle. All began during the founding of Rome about the same time our clan was encountering the Viking raids. The myth of Romulus and Romulus...all a reality for our race. The Lupus Sanguis Chalice, that can save a werewolf's life, made from the bone and blood of the original she-wolf, came from that era."

I remained silent, too stunned to answer at the realization of all there was in the world I had not been party to. *Until now.*

"You need to promise me something, angel."

Logan's tone changed. His voice filled with something new, a different note I had never heard him use before.

"What is it?" I turned to look him in the eye. I could clearly see he was worried and that concern meant I had something to worry about too.

"I need you to swear you'll keep quiet about all this. Humans are not supposed to know we exist. It upsets the order of things."

"No kidding!" My frustration at being broadsided spilled out. "These past few minutes have been insane! I don't know whether I'm coming or going—it's crazy!"

"I'm sorry you've been upset by all this. That was not my intention. I only wanted to save you from the kidnappers. To bring you home safe and sound." A sincere earnestness colored his words.

"Thank you."

"No thanks necessary. I would go to the ends of the earth to protect you. That's who I am."

"Are all of your clan like this?"

"Aye." He nodded, the truth of it in his face as a glimpse of the past appeared, his face ancient and timeless with the wisdom of the ages clear in his liquid green eyes. The playful playboy had long vanished and a warrior stood at my side, ready to protect his woman. He kept glancing at the roadway, perhaps making sure the men who had abducted me weren't bearing down on us. We needed to go, but first I needed to know more, to make some sense of things.

His natural use of the ancient *aye* helped convince me more that this was all too real.

"Where do we go from here?" The time of revelation had passed. Now we needed a plan.

"You mean us?" He zeroed in on my face, his eyes questioning me.

"I mean where does this leave us going forward? Now that I know things I shouldn't about who you are? About your clan?" A new worry had surfaced. Had I been saved by Logan only to face new trials? This precious, mind-blowing information had to come with some cost, right? I lived in that domain and I had understood the price paid for understanding. People fought tooth and nail to reach the apex of the ivory tower. The knowledge I now possessed was beyond priceless.

"I will protect you at any cost." His words came out strong.

"Are you saying there's a cost to you for me knowing this? Are you in any danger?"

"No. Why, would that worry you?" His eyes bore into mine.

"Of course! The man I've been spending time with being in danger because of me? Sure, that's a huge issue for me." Thinking of Logan being hurt any more than he already was made my throat tighten.

"You never have to worry about me. I can take care of myself. You're the one who needs protecting, not me. But thank you for caring."

"Well, I do care. But where do we go from here?" Frustration at the unknown made me want to throw something or have a hissy fit. My life was normally so ordered, so staid, maybe boring at times, but at least I knew what the deal was.

"If you can swear an oath, make a promise in blood, never to divulge this information, maybe we can salvage things?"

"If not?"

He shook his head. "Revealing what you know would be dangerous to my family. And to all the houses and clans of werewolves around the world. Something I would try my best not to let happen."

"What? Would you abduct me too?"

"As good as that sounds, being forced to spend all my life with you, I couldn't do that to you. You have to be with me of your own volition, your own will. But something will have to be done." His expression stilled, making my heart rate jack up.

"What do they do?" Obviously, this had to have happened before. There had to be some kind of a reasonable remedy without giving a blood oath. I shuddered at the idea. Blood was not my thing. I couldn't even stand the thought of a needle drawing blood.

"We hire a vampire to wipe your mind clean of the events that revealed us to you."

"What. The. Fuck!" Stunned, I just sat there and tried to squeeze air back into my lungs.

Chapter Twenty

Logan

"I could never harm you," I said, trying to reassure my angel. Surely, she understood that much at least now. I had done all I could to save her and would do so for all our time on this earth.

"But you would let a freakin' vampire do something to my mind? Wait! They exist too?" Her eyes widened by shock, her cheeks going a shade paler, she just shook her head slowly as if unable to process the information.

"No choice, really. Either you become one of us or we have to make you forget we exist." That option was the worst. I wanted her to come freely to me. To desire to be with me. Wishing I had had more time before it came to this, I sat quietly, letting her take it all in. I thought I would have weeks to slowly persuade her of things, not make her face everything so abruptly.

"Wait! That's an option? Becoming a werewolf?"

"Yes." Thoughts of my angel being just like me, wanting to be one of us... That idea roared up in my mind, blowing every other thought clear out of my head. Her and I, a mated pair, sharing everything together. Would she choose us? It would be perfect. And if she had any problems shifting, there was the chalice to ease her way.

The Lupus Sanguis Chalice, or wolf blood chalice, had been discovered buried in Alaska by the Luceres twins, of all places, and heralded a new beginning for all of us. Human mates were now protected from the change. Before its discovery, many mates died trying to shift to wolf. A tragedy beyond comprehension for any Forever Mate. When a fated one died, the soul of the other mate withered away. Rejection was also a tragic path that did not bear thinking about. *Too painful and final.*

"We have to go!" I spotted the men pursuing us turning off the highway, interrupting my thoughts.

We raced for the van and I jumped into the driver's seat before Justine could, ignoring the pain while I scrambled in behind the wheel, gunning the motor. I took off so quickly I was thrown back against the seat, not taking the time to buckle myself in.

"Seat belt," I half-shouted at her. "And hang on!"

We weaved our way down the highway, headed for the Glitter Palace. If I could lose them in traffic, we could hide out in the hotel while our security team dealt with them. Apparently, they hadn't learned their lesson yet, hadn't realized they were lucky to still be alive. *Keep this up and that option was right off the table.*

"If I were a werewolf, I could better protect myself, right?"

Stunned by her astuteness considering all she had undergone today, I nodded, keeping my focus dead ahead.

"Yes, the best option in my humble opinion."

"There's nothing humble about you, Logan Creig."

Too busy concentrating to respond, I stomped on the gas pedal. The vehicle shot ahead, all cylinders firing, the motor loud and impressive. The abrupt movement thrust Justine backward in the passenger seat, G forces pinning her down.

She stared at the roadway, her face pale as I directed us through the minefield of traffic, like we were in the Indie 500. The van rocked to the side as I made a swift maneuver around a large semi-truck in the way then lurched again, righting itself. Justine grabbed the dash, her fingers clenched tight.

We were leaving the black SUV behind, incapable of keeping up with my driving skills, honed by long hours of practice at the hands of the Lycan Security Force. They offered multiple courses at the school near London, England, in everything imaginable to protect our own. I'd earned one of the highest scores ever on my final test. Maybe Justine had a point. Humbleness was not my forte. But then what person or supernatural in this world can exist without a healthy dose of ego for protection against the inevitable knocks of life?

"What other superpowers does becoming like one of you endow a human being with?"

Was she really considering the option and not just playing with me, giving me hope?

"I already mentioned the extra strength, endurance, fast healing and improved eyesight, right?" I pressed my foot down harder on the gas pedal, hitting a more open stretch of roadway, enjoying the sensation of flying down the highway with my angel at my side. Even the pain of my wounds had lessened. "You can add telepathy between mates. Also between clan members when security demands it. Excellent night vision. Natural weapons when you're in wolf form like claws and sharp teeth. Enhanced smell, which came in useful today when I tracked you down."

"I am grateful. I'm sorry. I haven't thanked you yet for saving my ass."

"You're welcome," I said. "But no need to. I just acted on instinct. There was no time to think things out. When I couldn't find you right after the fire alarm, I began my search at the prop room and got there in time to see the van leaving. Fucking good luck on my part."

"Otherwise, who knows what might have happened?" She looked pensive, a frown creasing her forehead. "What's shifting like?"

"The best! Well, not better than sex, of course."

I chanced a quick look at her. Her lips quirked up at the corners. "It would be hard to beat the sex, yes."

I was encouraged to see her mood lighten and I rushed to add more positives. "When you're wolf, the world reduces to its simplest form. Life becomes exhilarating. The amazing scents and images are far more powerful. Running on four limbs has to be tried to be believed. You feel invincible, like there's nothing you can't do."

"Well, that doesn't suck."

"No, it doesn't." I turned and gave her my most charming smile.

"Don't do that."

"What?" Confused, I wanted to lock eyes with her but kept my senses and paid attention to traffic.

"Try to manipulate me. Just be your sincere self. You're a good man, Logan, and you don't need to be anyone but you. That's the man I like. The man I admire."

She'd said like, not love. That hurt. But it was also good to hear that she wanted me for me. Not that smooth-talking wolf that all the ladies wanted for a night. It was something to build on. But we had bigger problems right now. I needed to find out who those guys were that had taken my angel. Put a stop to it. Report the incident. Then get back to work. The movie was not going to direct itself.

"How long do I have to make a decision?"

I didn't need to ask what she meant. The woman had a clever, decisive mind, no doubt about it. Justine was the whole deal, beautiful, passionate and inquisitive by nature. It was what drew me to her, that insatiable lust for life.

"Sooner is better than later."

"I can't get my mind around how every molecule in a body can be manipulated in such a way as to become another species. That just defies explanation."

"As you are most likely aware, in physics, energy is never lost. Werewolves became altered at the quantum level due to their special DNA. But when I shift, I do get a glimpse of another world just before bouncing back to ours in my new form. It's a parallel realm close to ours. Probably one of the eleven dimensions that the scientific community postulates about in theory."

"So you were born that way? And how do I get that DNA?"

"Through saliva."

"A bite, you mean. So, it's all true. That's how one gets infected."

I bristled. "It's not an infection like the damn plague. It's an endowment. A positive."

"There's got to be a downside, right? Everything has a cost."

There was that logical part of her brain at work. I wanted to take her in my arms, kiss all that skepticism away and have her agree on the spot to my bite. *Make her mine forever. Brand her.*

"If you think feeling the urge to shift—okay, sometimes at inconvenient times—a negative." I paused, paying attention to arriving at the Glitter Palace. I would normally choose valet parking, but today was no normal day. I was driving a stolen van filled with priceless artifacts with a woman who had been kidnapped. I needed to keep a low profile.

I turned down a side street and parked in the alley near the door to the prop room. I didn't have my phone on me, having lost it in the shift.

"Do you have your phone?" I asked Justine.

She scrambled to pull it from a pocket, handing it over.

I texted security to meet us ASAP. I wanted these artifacts safely inside. And twenty-four-hour surveillance. This was *never* going to happen again on my watch.

Chapter Twenty-One

Justine

There was a third option on the table.

Run. Take off for the hills and never look back. But then I would be giving up my profession as I would need to change my name to disappear. Lose my friendship with Marnie. Everything that mattered in my life. Complicated didn't half cover it.

And what about Logan? I might not have known him long, but his imprint in my life was gigantic. I was drawn to him in so many ways. Some of it was inexplicable. Especially considering we were actually of a different species. *Wait, does that mean angels are real?* Thoughts of the precious Infinity Egg sitting behind me in the back of the van and the wings etched on its surface rising up behind one of the characters claimed my attention for a moment. *Are there angels on Earth among us?* If what Logan had been saying about werewolves was all true — I had no reason to doubt him considering what I had seen and experienced today —

then the other supernaturals also existed. *Oh, to meet an angel.* The very thought blew me away.

Get a hold of yourself. You got bigger worries than angels. A vampire might very well be sent to wipe your mind clean. The thought frightened me to the core. I shivered. Would I lose all the amazing information I had been given this week? That would be a stunning loss. Oh crap, Cynthia Dixon knew about the Infinity Egg! Not as much as me, but enough to know that the material it was made of did not exist on Earth. Would her mind need to be wiped clean as well? And exactly how clean did they make it?

We had just pulled up outside the alley alongside the prop room door when it all hit me. The logistics of this thing had gotten right out of control.

"Do you have your phone on you?" Logan asked. I dug it out of my pocket on autopilot and handed it over. Thoughts were streaming through my brain nonstop. I rubbed my forehead as a headache bloomed.

"What about Professor Cynthia Dixon?" I had to ask.

"What about her?" Logan narrowed his eyes.

"She knows about the Infinity Egg. That it's not made of any substance known on Earth. Is that a problem?"

He pursed his lips. "Maybe. She knows nothing about its use?"

"Just that when a human being touches it, it opens and gives that little speech."

"Nothing about other supernaturals?"

I shook my head. "No."

"Would she kick up a fuss if she never gets to see it again, do you think?"

"She wanted to run more tests."

"What if it disappeared in the robbery? The one thing that we didn't get back? Hmm, that might work."

I took a deep breath. "Thank you."

"For what?"

"For not wanting to mind wipe her or some horrible thing like that."

"I'm not a monster, Justine. Just loyal to my clan. I want them to stay safe. And I don't make the rules."

"But you follow them, at the expense of others."

"What would you have me do?"

He sounded impatient now, angry or hurt at my response.

"Bring it all out into the open. This is the perfect opportunity. You have a lot to offer this world —"

"Let me stop you right there. That's *never* going to happen. We haven't hidden who we are since the beginning of time for no reason. It's to protect everything we have. You need to accept that some things are never going to change. This is written in stone. The number-one pack rule is the existence of our kind must *never* be revealed. Followed by the second rule, the alpha always protects his mate and his offspring with his life."

His voice was cold, authoritarian, not at all like his usual tone. He handed me back my phone and I held on to it like it was a lifeline. Hurt consumed me, making me want to lash out. He had just rejected my attempt to help him and his clan. To think I had thought it fun to call him *sir*. Reason had left the damn building.

"Security is here. I have to help. We'll talk about this later."

"Damn right we will." I jumped out of the van. I was angrier than I had ever been before, ignoring the fact I was most likely in shock as well. He was being such a gigantic pain in my ass. The world would embrace such amazing wonders as werewolves and vampires, not to mention angels and a whole host of other supernaturals. Wouldn't it? They had to be at least half as fascinated as I was. And I was fascinated to the core. Every nerve fiber and cell in my body tingled with it, excited under the pissed-off feeling of things out of my control.

Yes. I needed to step back from this situation. Clear my head. I had been letting passion and lust control me. Not my usual way to operate. That was the problem. A fresh perspective was in order.

Marnie. I worked the keyboard on my phone, my thumbs flying. But the call went to voice mail. Instead of leaving a message, I sent a text asking her to get back to me ASAP.

In the meantime, I was getting the hell out of here. Logan was busy helping the security men to haul the final artifacts inside. Fortunately, the Infinity Egg was also unharmed from our wild chase through traffic. But now was the perfect time for me to make a quick getaway. I waited until he stepped back out of view, his arms full, then I turned and walked away.

I drove home on autopilot, my mind reeling with the implications and complications of what I now knew about the world. I needed a drink in the worst way. Or ten.

As soon as I was in the door, I grabbed the first wine I found chilled in the refrigerator. I drank from the bottle, not even bothering with a glass. Our first real fight. And it was about him being a werewolf? *Fucking crazy.* Well, I couldn't go back to the set. Maybe more of them were werewolves? Was it even safe?

I hiccuped, the too-cold wine making my esophagus spasm. I set it aside after a couple of swallows. I was hyperventilating. Holding my breath, I willed my body to calm down. Tears filled my eyes. Best boyfriend I'd ever had and he turned out to be unattainable. I just couldn't imagine myself being bitten and turned into a wolf. I couldn't even handle blood, for heaven's sake. I might be feisty about a lot of things, but I really didn't want to test that phobia that had made itself known at eighteen when I'd had blood drawn for the first time.

Add hemophobia to the list of irrational fears. *But being scared shitless of werewolves couldn't really be classified as a phobia once you knew they were real, right?* I sank onto the couch, thought of drinking the wine abandoned. That would just make the situation worse, getting drunk. *Christ, what a clusterfuck.*

My phone buzzed. Relieved, I answered it after checking it was Marnie on the other end. Last person I wanted to talk to right now was Logan.

"Hey, how's it going?" she asked, her cheerful tone breaking through all my defenses.

"Not so good. We had a *big* fight." Then I realized I couldn't really tell her what was really wrong between Logan and me. Not if I wanted to keep her safe.

"Aww, shit, sorry to hear that. Deal breaker?"

"Maybe." I hiccuped again.

"Tell your captain. I'm done swabbing the decks for today. In fact, why don't I come over and we can commiserate together? Watch a silly movie?"

I laughed in spite of my troubles. "No, I'm fine. I just need to ponder things, think about where I'm going. He's not who I thought he was." *No kidding, he's a man* and *a wolf.*

"If you're sure? But, yeah, when the shine comes off, they never are. That was kind of a short honeymoon, but at least you got your feet wet. And other parts."

"You're so bad. But yeah, the sex was off the charts."

"Sometimes that's all it is. There's nothing else in common to help a couple make it through the transition to being in love."

"Well, we did have some things in common other than the bedroom."

"Like?"

"He's loyal to a fault to his family and friends."

"I didn't know that was possible," Marnie mused. "Did he put them first over you? Is that what this is all about?"

"Yeah, he did." The ultimatum hurt. *Turn yourself into a werewolf or have your mind blanked to keep his family and clan safe. I mean, who has to make that impossible choice?*

"Well, he has known them far longer than he's known you. Loyalty is a good trait. You have it in spades yourself."

"Not helping." Of course, she couldn't help me because I couldn't tell her what was wrong. To think how safe my former life was. Boring, okay, but safe. Though to his credit, Logan had promised to protect me. But could he really, from an army of supernaturals out to get my head? I shuddered, shaky and off balance, remembering the rescue. He'd damn near taken their heads off. Okay, he was protective, I'll give him that. "He does try to shield me from others."

"In a good way? Like standing up for you in a confrontation? If you can't tell me specifics, at least tell me that."

"Definitely." At least when it involved outsiders. I didn't know what would have happened if he hadn't intervened with those horrible gangsters. But then I wouldn't have been in the fix in the first place if he hadn't insisted on my being his antiquities expert.

"That's good then. Not like he's letting anyone take advantage of you."

But is it enough? An idea sprang into my mind and I pounced on it. "Say, do you still have access to your parents' cabin? I need to get away, take a day or two to clear my head. That's if the offer is still on the table?"

"Of course it is. When do you want to go?"

"Tonight, if possible. Can I swing by and pick up the keys?"

"Sure. There's one other thing I hesitate to mention. I'm sorry to be the bearer of bad news, but knowledge will keep you forewarned, right?"

"Spill."

"It's Jane." Marnie cleared her throat. "She's suing you for breach of contract."

"*What?*"

"Yeah, that's what I said. But apparently you ruined her wedding by leaving early. Says she missed out on getting some photos of you in candid poses she wanted for her album she was gifting the bridesmaids."

"I thought those contracts she made us sign were a joke. Not the real thing." Jane had brought out the sheets of paper when she invited us to be in her wedding party, plied us with champagne and had us sign on the dotted line. We'd all laughed, thinking it a lark.

"I kid you not, but I'm working on talking her out of it. Soon as I have some dirt on her, she's so going to drop that suit. Okay, see you in ten?"

"Ahh, yeah, be right there. Just got to pack a bag." Jane was suing *me*? Since when had the world gone so totally bonkers? But yeah, Marnie would have my back.

I hurried into the bedroom and threw a few things in an overnight bag, agitated and thoroughly pissed. Surely she wouldn't be successful in her bid to elicit funds from me over not living up to her standards as a bridesmaid? God, I needed to get away. I raced to the bathroom and grabbed a few toiletry items. A couple of days to clear my head wasn't asking much, considering what I had been through this past week.

Chapter Twenty-Two

Logan

"Okay, that's everything." The biggest prize, the artifact Justine called the Infinity Egg, was safely packed in a crate, ready to be shipped to the Highlands on the next private flight home in the morning. Finn was personally taking care of it, which meant no more worries about it on my part. I hurried back outside to escort Justine and found the van empty. Where was she? I reached for my phone and remembered I'd lost it in the confrontation with the gangsters.

"*Damn it.*" I stomped back into the prop room and strode up to the first security guard available.

"I need your phone." If I couldn't locate her, I would have to make The Call. Last thing I wanted to do on this earth was put Justine at risk by telling my brothers and Cristaldo what had happened. That she was a loose cannon out there knowing all about our kind. It put everything that mattered most in the world to me at risk — my clan and my angel.

The man handed it over without a word. I punched in Justine's number and waited and waited some more. It went to voice mail and I barked out my message. "Where are you, angel? Is everything all right? If I don't hear from you in the next five minutes, I'm heading over to check your place. Call me."

We'd just been through a war together and she upped and vanished. My stomach clenched into a fist. She had to know how worried I would be. Why would she do such a thing? *God, please don't let anything happen to her.* Why hadn't I been paying closer attention? But she'd been sitting quietly, locked in the front seat of the van while we unloaded the stash, as safe as I could make her. Was I failing in that regard? The thought hurt like a son of a bitch.

"I'll see you get your cell back ASAP, and I'll be back soon. Tell the others I have an errand to run," I ordered the guard.

The guard nodded and I jumped back in the van, uncaring that I was still wearing the overalls and needed a shower more than anything.

Then my borrowed phone buzzed. *Justine.* I read the text.

I'm fine. Please, give me some space. I need to think about things. I'll call you soon. I promise I won't say anything to anyone about what I know.

Stymied, I stopped and considered my options. Showing up at her house stinking of wolf and reeking of blood probably wasn't the best idea I've ever had. She was right, as much as I didn't want to admit it. She did need time to clear her head. A lot had happened in a very short period. Most people would be reeling, feeling they were on uncertain ground. Best to give her the night at least, then speak with her in the positive light of a new day. I had her word she would respect our kind and not say anything and I believed her. I might be in trouble for this, but I would give her a few hours' grace.

But even the mere thought of a short separation hurt. *The wolf-pull.* One thing though—she'd feel it too, if she was truly my Forever Mate. That intense longing for the other that could never be satisfied until in their company. The only thing for it was to go ahead with the night shoot and try my best not to dwell on the situation.

That in mind, I headed upstairs for a shower, first texting security from a backup cell phone I kept on hand to stay posted outside her house to make sure she was kept safe.

Back in the saddle of the dolly thirty minutes later behind the camera operator, I was soon engrossed in my work. The heist part of the movie needed to be filmed in the middle of the night to avoid the crowds, meaning we had scant hours until dawn to complete the first section of it on the storyboard.

Just before we began filming, my phone vibrated, indicating an incoming text.

Located outside house. Everything quiet. Lights off.

I'd told the four-man team to check in on the hour to give me an update. *Good.* Now I could get down to it. It didn't mean I didn't miss my angel's presence like a son of a bitch on camera and off, but at least I knew she was safe and resting, hopefully gaining a new perspective. We would find our way through this small roadblock in short order. Every fated mate had issues at first, at least according to Lachlan. I'd called him earlier tonight, asking for him to send me a certain something that should end Justine's worries about my commitment to her, that should prove it was as real as it came.

"Action!" I called and we were off and running.

By dawn, we had precious moments of cinema history in the can and it was time to head up to my suite for a fresh grooming, grab a bouquet of blossoms and be with Justine when she woke up. What was her favorite flower? *So much I want to learn about her.* A lifetime wouldn't be near enough.

Hair dripping wet and a towel tied around my waist, I checked my messages. Still nothing. Being out of communication was brutal, but she was most likely still sleeping. I should be there with her, wanting nothing more than to hold her in my arms and share how very, very precious she was to me. Maybe it was time to let her know how I had fallen for her from the first moment I saw her shining under the lights of the casino, the scent of roses teasing me as it had ever since. What I could see in her, the potential for us to share an amazing future together—it was everything now.

I dried off and dressed in a dark suit and pale green dress shirt without a tie, wanting to be approachable. I'd pick up flowers in the gift shop on my way out. I slipped the small midnight-blue velvet box expressed overnight from Castle Creigbourne and containing a family heirloom in my pocket and picked up my car keys.

Time to win my fair lady.

Justine

I woke disorientated and groggy. Where was I? Then images of the day before came rushing in. The abduction. The crazy aftermath. The hour-and-a-half drive through deserted streets and into the countryside to reach Marnie's family retreat on the mountainside overlooking Lake Mead.

Apparently, I'd lain down on the sofa last night instead of finding a bed. My back complained with the knowledge. I ignored it and stumbled across the living room floor to check out the panoramic view the place was famous for, to be stunned by the beauty of the sunrise sending fingers of deep pink and bright yellow across the landscape. Uplifting didn't begin to cover it as ancient rockfaces turned to sheets of molten gold.

I stood there, drinking in the magic of creation. A miracle that I rarely took a single moment to revere. That needed to change. Though not so much as rethinking my priorities, it seemed. Maybe trying to obtain a full professorship was too costly, if it meant having to be exposed to such events as yesterday. Not that I hadn't enjoyed working with the movie people, like Skye and the others. But being abducted, held by criminals, then watching what Logan had done to rescue me — that was all too much.

And yet, in the end, he had saved me. And in doing so exposed himself and one of the world's biggest secrets. What would his fellow clansmen think of that? Would they blame him? That thought made me squirm. I didn't want that to happen. *Not fair to him, not at all.* Logan cared about others. That was obvious from the way he treated everyone on set to how he treated me every moment of the day and night.

But this aftermath, this was bad karma that I didn't know how to fix. I thought of the options again. I knew at that moment that I must be feeling more for Logan than I cared to admit. Otherwise, why make a choice? I could just go straight to the police, right? But, *big* but, would they take me seriously? Spouting a story about werewolves and other supernaturals existing here on Earth since the time of the Egyptians? No. That wasn't a good choice if I didn't want to be thrown directly into the looney bin. Well, I couldn't just hide. That also rubbed me the wrong way.

But choose, werewolf or mind wipe? Who can do that? One came with no knowledge of what I had been through. The other with a man attached. How serious was Logan? Would I become a werewolf — big if — only to find him looking to charm another? I'd give him one thing. He had been changing. He'd sent those annoying twins home when they'd overstepped boundaries and hadn't even glanced at another woman in my presence. And just as importantly, how serious was I? I wasn't looking for a man, especially one with all of Logan's baggage, and yet here he was affecting my life on so many levels. The extreme lust had caused me to lower my boundaries and I was uncertain if that was a good thing or the worst choice I'd ever made.

Well, enough of this. I needed coffee and lots of it. I prayed that someone had left a tin on their last trip to Lake Mead, but had no such luck when I searched the kitchen cabinets. I'd have to venture into Boulder City for supplies. Not bothering to shower, I pulled my hair into a messy bun, donned a loose-fitting sundress — the thermometer was already rising — and picked up my car fob. There were two main temperatures in the desert — too cold at night and too hot during the day.

The short drive into the city was scenic, all rough-hewn boulders and big views. Mirages appeared in the distance, hovering on the horizon, shimmering lights on the land's surface that created a kaleidoscope of wafting rainbow colors rising on thermal drafts. *Pretty amazing.* I suddenly wished Logan was here to share in the beauty of the images. He'd appreciate them. His sensitivity to light and shadow was phenomenal.

What do wolves see? Feel? The thoughts jumped into my mind unbidden. If one wanted the sense of pure freedom, escape from the bounds of a controlling society, that was one way of getting there.

The sight of a coffee shop caused me to scramble to locate a parking spot nearby then get into line behind others needing their own early morning caffeine fix. A mug of hot black coffee in hand, I found a window seat and plunked down.

My phone buzzed and I glanced at the caller. Logan. I dithered, unsure. But then relented, knowing he would only worry if I didn't answer.

"Justine! Where are you? I'm at your house and you're not here."

His voice did indeed sound concerned. I swallowed.

"I had to get away. I'm sorry I worried you. I'm fine, really."

"You don't sound fine. Tell me where you are and I'll come get you."

"No. That's not a good idea. I want time alone — to think. Please, I'm fine. I'll be back in a day or two."

"There's something important I wanted to ask you, but not over the phone. You sure you're okay?"

I closed my eyes. His voice rumbled through me, touching off a host of sensations, mostly pleasant. Too pleasant. I wanted to feel his arms around me in the worst way. But I would not be forced into making a decision that was life-changing without a lot of time to think it through.

"You threw me a curve ball with yesterday's revelations. And I need time to process it all." I might as well be honest. "I won't be rushed and I won't be threatened."

"Who's threatening you?" His tone was steely, like the threat was external. It wasn't. It was my worry over how his clan would react to an outsider knowing of their existence that had me feeling the most worried.

"The fact that I only have two choices, that's a huge problem." Suddenly I wanted to talk about all this in person. But then we would be jumping into bed too quickly and not hashing out our differences. This was the best way. The only way I was going to have perspective was keeping away for now. Then why was it so difficult being away from him?

"I never meant for you to feel that way. I want to enhance your life, make sure you have the best of everything, that each day is lived to its fullness." He cleared his throat. "Okay, I'll do whatever possible to make sure none of this comes back on you. I won't tell my family about what you know. If you can promise me not to tell anyone about our existence."

"But won't that get you in trouble if that's ever discovered—that you didn't warn them about me?"

"If they knew, yes. But your promise is all I need. I believe in you. I trust you. I choose you."

I was stunned into silence. An alpha male saying such a thing, leaving himself vulnerable—I was certain it was unprecedented among his peers. It made me respect him all the more.

"I'll call you soon," I said, remembering to breathe.

"You're missed on set as well. Skye said to say hello."

"Hello back." I swallowed, not really wanting to hang up but knowing I must. I missed Logan with every fiber of my being, but I had to be sure. I wasn't a person who normally looked for a sign from the universe to know what they should do, but, right now, I'd appreciate one.

As if Logan knew I couldn't be the one to hang up, the line went dead as he made the decision for us. The silence hurt and I fumbled with the phone, nearly dropping it on the floor.

My phone immediately rang again.

"Logan?" I said, my heart leaping with joy imagining he had called me back right away that I didn't check the incoming number.

"No, sugar tits. I'm not your boyfriend unless you want me to be," the man on the other end said in a cold voice that sent terror racing through every cell in my body. "We want the artifact. The Infinity Egg."

"Who are you?" I managed to squeak out. "How did you get this number?"

"You know who we are. And you know we can get to you anytime we want to. So, two choices, as I see it. Hand it over or tell us where it is if you want everything you care about to stay safe."

This was no idle threat. My throat dry, my mind refused to accept it all.

"What will it be, Professor? You need more proof of what we can do? How easily we can find you? Or anyone you care about?"

I took a breath. If they really knew where I was, they would be here already, my logical brain stated. They didn't know anything about this place. But what about the movie crew? Well, some were likely werewolves, I guessed, thinking of all the green-colored eyes. Did these people know who they were dealing with? Or were they some kind of supernaturals too? That thought was the most terrifying of all, thinking of all the choices the Infinity Egg suggested on its skin.

"Are you part of that weird group, Creation's Witnesses?" I asked, to buy time and keep myself from jumping into the deep end and drowning.

Silence.

"You have twenty-four hours to deliver the item to us. We'll be in touch with particulars."

The line went dead.

If I needed proof of which way the wind was blowing, this was it. Going back to Logan wasn't an option now. As much as the idea hurt, more than I wanted to admit, feeling the pain spike through me, we needed to stay as far away from each other as possible. Insanity was winning the day. Forces were at work to harm both of us. *God, I wish I knew who these Creation's Witnesses really are.* What kind of monster were they? What could they do to us?

My hands trembling and my heart pounding, I fired off a quick text to Logan before I could change my mind.

Don't try to find me. You will never see me again. This is for your own good. Stay safe.

Chapter Twenty-Three

Logan

I discovered that promising Justine I would not hold her feet to the fire over her knowing about my clan's unique situation *and* feeling comfortable with whatever her final decision about us was were two different things. I wanted her to choose a life spent as equals. How could I help her see that becoming a she-wolf would only enhance her life? All the money and resources in the world were nothing but ash if she wasn't by my side.

As the hours went by and my body missed hers to the point that even breathing felt like a chore without her, the breaking point came during the final shoot of the night.

"Cut!"

"We need to redo that scene. One of the actors muffed their line," Connor said, stretching his arms over his head to relieve the ache in his shoulders.

"No, I'm done tonight. We'll pick it up tomorrow night. I have to go out of town."

"The schedule—I hate to say this and I'm sure you don't need reminding—but it's tight, Logan. I'd hoped to begin tomorrow at noon. And Justine Bell will be back by then, right? We need her for some of the heist shots as well. So far, no time has been lost, but that's coming to an end."

"Excuse me. I have to go. I'll call you soon as I know more."

Connor didn't look happy about it, but he had the common sense to stop talking and let me walk away. Damn it, I didn't like letting my people down, but I couldn't go on like this. I had to see Justine, to find out where her mind was at. I had her address on my phone from the man I'd paid a small fortune to discover it, and I intended to use it. Sure, I'd promised to give her time to think, but how much time does a woman in love need?

I took out my phone and checked if I had missed anything while I'd been working. Seeing a text from Justine, I read it, then read it again, because my mind and my heart could not accept what they were seeing.

Don't try to find me. You will never see me again. This is for your own good. Stay safe.

Justine

The day had passed in a haze, my mind going round and round in an ever-tighter loop. I was dizzy and exhausted from too much coffee and no food, and my appetite had vanished, I lay on the sofa for hours and tried to watch an old movie, but I couldn't follow the simple plot to save my soul.

I got up and stumbled to the window to watch the sliver of a moon looming over Lake Mead. It called to me tonight. So ancient and mystical. I sensed all the humans and creatures that had come before me, that all of them had looked up during their lives and had been touched by that same moon call. One constant in life.

Yes.

I had made the right decision earlier tonight.

I wasn't going to go back to Vegas anytime soon. It was unsafe. For me and those I cared about. For fuck's sake, supernaturals were pursuing me at every quarter! I wanted order in my life, not the unknown. It was why I'd chosen a quiet life in the first place, far away from temptations like Logan. *Better to live without excitement than never knowing for certain what's around the next bend in the road.* My father had deserted us because he wanted that, greedy for more.

It was better to give up now than have my heart broken worse later. Not to mention, I didn't want another run-in with any other creature or monster. Was it going to be like Pandora's Box, the Infinity Egg? A new paranormal showing up periodically? I couldn't have that, no fucking way. At least if I stayed away, then I called it, stayed in control.

A knock on the door startled the living daylights out of me. I dropped the water bottle I was holding. It bounced on the hardwood floor and I leaned over and picked it up. Who was here? Had Marnie forgotten that one of her other relatives was expected?

I glanced at the clock over the fireplace, noting it was three in the morning.

Uncomfortable with answering the door with being a female all alone in the middle of the night, I moved to stand in front of it and called out, "Who is it?"

"Logan."

Damn it. No. He knew where I stood. That we were over. *Just accept it already.*

I hesitated, not wanting to face him. *Be brave, Justine. You know what you have to do.*

"I need to talk to you."

Nothing for it. I opened the door, bracing myself. I crossed my arms and hugged them around my body, trying to warm up. He looked a bit disheveled as well, his thick hair coming loose from its leather tie. He needed food and drink and a proper rest just like me. *Yeah. Breaking up is a bitch.*

"Can I come in?"

I stood my ground. No good could come of this.

"Please, angel. We need to talk."

I stepped aside. Nothing he could say would change my mind, of course. I had to be the strong one here, to see things for what they were.

"Would you like something to drink?" We sounded so formal, uncomfortable, uncertain for the first time ever around each other.

"No. I'm good. I just needed to see for myself that you're doing okay. You vanished so quickly yesterday. I was worried. I shut down the shoot early to come."

"You didn't have to do that. You got my text, right? You know where I stand."

The silence stretched between us as I searched for the words that would soften what I had to say. Why was he making me do this? Say these painful things? "I've made up my mind. We're two different people. Hell, we're not even the same species. I'm sorry. That's not fair." The hurt on his face pained me. "But you know what I mean."

"We can fix it. We're only weeks away from hunter's moon...an auspicious time to become a wolf."

The hope in his face took my breath clear away. He cared deeply. That was obvious. Doubts about breaking up with him rose to the surface again. *No.* I had made my decision abundantly clear. Going back on it would only be more painful in the long run. The universe was against us. He didn't even know how much that was true. I hadn't shared anything about Creation's Witnesses, how our being together was dangerous on so many levels. But this wasn't the time to bring all that up, hurtful enough as it was.

I shook my head. "No. That's not going to happen. And don't worry—I have no intention of *ever* telling anybody anything about who you really are. My lips are sealed for all time. I'll even take a blood oath if that helps." I managed to avoid shuddering at the word blood, but Logan was astute—he didn't miss my reaction by the look on his face.

"You're worried about the process of becoming a wolf? I can help you with that. It's not much really. Over in short order. But the benefits—beyond amazing. To feel the night air caress your fur as you race across the land… Nothing beats it. You sense all the ancient nature of things. Feel connected to eternal existence like never before."

"Not going to happen. I'm sorry, I apologize for getting your hopes up. I'm just too set in my ways. I don't want to live life on the edge. I chose a staid life on purpose."

"Where is that exciting, invigorating, amazing woman I met?" He looked more confused now than anything.

"I'm keeping her constrained. She's trouble." *Like my dad.*

"Is there anything I can say or do to change things?"

"No. I've made up my mind." *Only way to keep us and everything we care about safe.*

We stared at each other across the painful chasm that loomed at our feet. I'd come so far from calling him 'sir' that it seemed a lifetime ago. There was no going back to simpler times now.

Then he was gone, fleeing into the night. A single bright flash followed. Then a keening series of howls pierced the sky.

My heart constricted into a lead weight in my chest. *What have I done?*

Logan

My mate.
Rejected.
Me.

There was no coming back from that. I shrugged off my clothes, uncaring of any permanent damage, and shifted, the urge to escape paramount.

My paws chewed up the distance, finding scrabbling purchase on the uneven desert floor, chilled by the night. Uncaring of anything or even where I ended up, I let the sway of the moon course through me and lead the way into the darkest reaches of my soul.

The worst pain imaginable sliced through me, setting my blood on fire, the licks of hell in the burning pit. Like there was any other option. There was not. The pain…indescribable.

A series of unavoidable howls erupted periodically from my constricted chest and into my aching throat, interrupting the dead of the night. I needed my fellows, the fellowship. But they were too far away. Across the sea. Unable to help. Would I live through this night? Did it matter? To go on alone, without my angel…

Unthinkable.

I ignored the suffering of my paws being cut open on the rough ground, trailing blood behind me. The agony of losing everything overcame me. I stumbled in the dark, my soul trapped. Tortured.

How would this night end? None of that mattered now. My mind shut down, unable to bear what should not be. Wretched, a sudden new pain tore at my paw, making me unable to go on. I fell to the ground, overcome by grief and trapped by something not of my making.

Chapter Twenty-Four

Justine

I couldn't sleep. I couldn't eat. I couldn't drink. *What the living fuck is the matter with me?* I had done the right thing. The prudent thing. Why was the pain so bad it threatened to consume me?

I lay on the sofa and stared at the ceiling, too exhausted to bother moving. I should be making a plan. But I felt frozen, incapable of driving anywhere today or any day. I was certain Logan wasn't in Sin City anyway. Was he still out there, in the desert? I had no way of tracking him — obviously he had no phone on him. But I sensed he needed help. Who should I call?

Maybe Skye would know? He'd keyed his info into my phone. Uncaring of what time it was, I brought up his number and called him.

"What's up, girlfriend?"

"I need your help. Could you give me a contact number for Logan's family in Scotland? I think he needs them."

"What happened?"

I gave him an abbreviated version of the encounter, the sense there was no time to waste hastening my words.

"Okay. I think he's in trouble." He recited off a stream of numbers and, hanging up on Skye, I called the overseas number.

"Creigbourne." An officious alpha male voice came across the air all the way from the Scottish Highlands, clear as a bell in its confidence and tone. No doubt he was a Creig, born and bred.

"Ah, you don't know me, but my name is Justine Bell. I work with Logan Creig on his upcoming movie as a consultant. And as an actress now." Why was I babbling about such unimportant information? *Get to the point, Justine.* "Is there anyone there I can talk to? I think he needs help."

"What have you done to my brother?" he demanded, his tone gone cold as brittle ice.

"I'm not certain that's relevant."

"It is if you've broken his heart. Damn it, I warned him of traps set for the unwary. You know, you're all he can talk about when he calls me."

"Sorry, who are you?" *What the hell is he talking about? Traps. I never set out to trap anyone in my life.* Wait! Logan had mentioned me to his family? Maybe he was more serious than I knew and not the playboy anymore.

"Lachlan. His oldest brother. Where are you right now? I'm flying there straight away. If you are his Forever Mate as he's so dead certain you are, then he's in real trouble. Don't do anything. And don't make matters worse by going after him, if you're not prepared to be with him."

Who was he to dictate how things went between Logan and me?

Before I could come up with a proper retort, Lachlan continued, "My brother is a sensitive artist. And if you've hurt him as bad as I think you have, you'll have me to answer to. He was going to ask you to marry him. Did you know that? He even sent for a family heirloom to be delivered yesterday to the casino. The wedding ring, presented to our great-grandmother by our great grandfather, and worn for sixty plus years of marriage. A very special thistle ring held in high regard by our clan, thought to ensure a happy home."

I swallowed. "A Scots thistle ring. He was that serious. I thought—well—I don't know what I thought…" My voice trailed off. I was not just another notch on his belt, not that he had ever made me feel like that. It was more that I felt backed into a corner with choices no human has ever had to make. That cult-like group had only added to my doubts. Perhaps I should have shared their part in this with Logan. Maybe then he would have understood my position better. *But no time for that now.*

I reeled off the particulars of my location to Lachlan and promised to wait until he arrived.

Why had I rejected Logan? Really? Just because I was squeamish around blood is no reason at all. Because he offered me a too-exciting life and that upset the status quo? Did I really want to date the boring Brads of the world? Men who preferred their mother's company to mine?

Shame and guilt struck. Logan had been serious about me. Not like my father at all. How had I not seen that? He'd taken on gangsters to protect me, to bring me home safe and sound. Exposed himself to pain and suffering. And now he was out there in the dark, alone and discouraged. I had to fix this. Damn those Creation's Witnesses all to hell!

Energized, I jumped to my feet. I had to go to him despite what his protective older brother cautioned. He needed me and I'd let him down. *This is all on me.* He was the one most invested in us. I had to find him, let him know how I really felt. That I had fallen in love with him. Everything else could be figured out from there.

But how to find him? It was still a couple of hours until dawn and too dark outside for human eyes. I moved to the kitchen and yanked out drawers, searching for a flashlight, knocking things about in my frantic search. *Eureka.* One lone silver-handled job was buried under a ton of knickknacks and junk. *Please, please have working batteries.* I clicked it on and a bright spotlight shone against the floor. *Thank you, God.*

I raced to the door and hurried into the night, holding the light like a beacon of hope before me. *I'm coming, Logan,* I called to him in my mind, wishing we were already mated and had telepathy. Right now, I'd give anything for that precious gift. Because I had a terrible feeling of dread washing over me every few seconds, whispering that something terrible was about to happen. I'd never had it before and it unnerved me to no end.

There. Tracks. He'd headed into the desert behind Lake Mead. Maybe I could catch up to him if he stopped to rest at some point.

A faint howling in the distance sent a series of chills snaking down my spine. But I had to chance it. *Nothing else for it.*

I made good time, half running across the landscape, stopping every few minutes to check for tracks. It was almost as if his animal tracks had a slight luminosity in the darkness. I didn't question it. Grateful for the help, I continued my sojourn around the edges of the lake, the sounds of water lapping at the manmade shore accompanying me.

I stumbled and fell over a rock, scraping my knees on the gravel strewn ground. Uncaring if I was bleeding or not, I continued, ignoring the starburst of pain. The light swinging wildly back and forth in my hand picked out a stunted tree here and there, dry sage brush and the occasional rusted can or discarded bottle.

Soon I had left the lake far behind and was climbing in elevation, my breath harsh in my ears as my body was pushed to the limit. Sweat dripped down my body despite the cooling temperatures. I wiped it from my eyes with the sleeve of my blouse, wishing I had thought to bring an emergency kit. What if he were lying hurt somewhere?

"Logan," I shouted every little while until my voice became hoarse and pain filled. How far had he gone? Then the ground began to descend, and I entered a canyon, the sides seeming to press in toward me. A sudden loud snap of something made of metal came above me on the ridgeline. I stopped moving to look upward. The loud snap was accompanied by a low, pained howl. What the hell? I began running toward the sound, scrambling upward in the darkness, holding on to bushes and uncaring of what I stepped on or what came at me.

"Logan?" I asked.

A terrible sight greeted me. A steel trap had been sprung, crushing his foreleg and pinning the huge creature to the ground. I tried getting closer but the wolf snapped at me, obviously in extreme pain. His eyes gleamed bright green, a wildness that I hadn't ever seen before scaring me to the core. Would he let me get closer?

"I'm sorry. I only want to help you. Please, let me help. I'm so sorry for everything." I ventured closer, but still felt uncertain as the wolf growled low in the chest, as if defying me to do anything.

I lowered myself to the ground and crept closer on my hands and knees, trying not to startle him. Did he even recognize me? Worry over the state of his mind heightened the moment, and tears began flowing down my cheeks. Had my rejection hurt him beyond repair? Oh my God, I couldn't live knowing that. Such an amazing man. If I had broken him, I had to be held accountable.

"Logan. It's me, Justine, your angel. I've come for you, to tell you that I love you and I never want to be parted from you."

I was close enough now to venture forth my hand. My fingers trembled. Would he bite me? That would be my just reward for sending him away. Unloved. Why had I not admitted it, embraced the life he was so graciously offering?

"I'm sorry I didn't tell you before. I was afraid. And other forces were interfering, testing me." With tears streaming down my face, I took a chance and showed him I had trust. I laid my hand on his snout, feeling the warmth.

My hand rested there for a second, the touch electric. Then he moved quickly, making my life rush before my eyes before his mouth came down on my hand. But it was only his tongue licking the palm, not teeth crushing flesh and bone.

I buried my face in his thick soft fur, letting it dry my tears. The fragrance of heather and maleness filled my nostrils, a heady potion. "I love you," I whispered. "Now and forever. Just like your great-grandparents. I see many decades ahead for us to celebrate our being together."

A low chuffing sound reached me and his green eyes glowed softer in the darkness.

"Can you shift? What do you need me to do?" I stared helplessly at the trap encasing his poor leg. Would he be able to walk again? How bad was it? I steeled myself, the guilt overwhelming me.

There was a slight shimmer of light, then nothing. He remained a wolf.

"What should I do?" I couldn't leave him to run for help. No human would venture close to a wolf. They might even harm him further.

"Maybe I can open the trap?" I bent over and began to examine how it worked. I wanted to throw up, but that was a luxury I could ill afford. Time was rushing by. Logan needed my help. Now.

"I have to get you free."

I tried pulling at the damn thing, forcing the jaws to open. But the metal was stiff, uncaring of who it held in its deadly grasp.

I screamed in frustration. Concentrate. *Use all your strength.* I applied myself again and again, pushing with all my might. I felt it give just a little, giving me hope. I forced my arms to work harder, trying another angle, sweat dripping in my eyes.

Then with a squawk of protest, it gave way enough to release his leg. He pulled it free and when I let go, the metal clamped on fresh air.

"Thank the Lord," I murmured. I examined the wound. I didn't like what I observed but just pressed my lips together and bore it. I tore off my top and wrapped it around the wound, tying the ends. "Can you stand?" There was no way I could carry him. He must have weighed two hundred pounds of solid muscle.

A brighter shimmer of light accompanied my words. Without the trap, maybe he could shift now? Then at least he could lean on me as we made our way back. If he were a man, someone would help us. But as a wolf, he would be suspect. I saw some of what he had been trying to tell me. Humans were quick to judge. They would shoot first and ask questions later. He had taken a terrible chance tracking me on the streets of Vegas. Someone could have shot him before he could save me, and there'd be no coming back from that. The guilt would have destroyed my life.

The light grew stronger and my hopes flared. Then a huge man and not a wolf lay on the ground. My beautiful man. I stared at him and our eyes locked, his filled with the same hope as my own.

"My angel," he said, a small smile curving his lips upward.

"My Logan. You're back."

He sat up and moved to check his leg, tying the makeshift bandage tighter.

"Shall we try standing up?" I asked.

"I need a stick or branch to support some of the weight. Could you look around for something?" His voice was roughened by the pain he was no doubt experiencing, but he remained stoic.

I appreciated any chance to help him and jumped to my feet, then played the flashlight back and forth, looking for anything that might work. A long, almost straight stick made of sturdy oak looked likely and I picked it up and handed it to Logan.

With my help, he was able to stand. Placing the stick cushioned by my pants that I quickly slipped off under his armpit, we began the slow walk back the way we'd come. It was going to take a long time, but I was determined to help every step of the way. Perhaps it would help relieve my guilt. Would Logan be left crippled? I couldn't go there, the thought too painful to contemplate.

Chapter Twenty-Five

Logan

The sun was just beginning to bloom over the edge of the Earth when Lake Mead came into view, sending rays of streaming light advancing on the land to caress the water. A brand-new day. A finer sight I could not imagine…unless it was the wonderful woman at my side.

She'd come. Found me on my darkest night. Said she shared my feelings. That love was in the cards for us. I had been right since the beginning — I'd seen something special in her, that lust for life that matched my own. Thoughts of my great-grandparents finding each other across the ocean filled my mind. Justine and I had followed them onto dry land.

"We're home, angel," I said, wanting her to share in my happiness.

"Are you going to be okay?" she asked, her beautiful face drawn with pain.

"Yes. The wound will knit, in time. It will scar, but I heal quickly." The steel of the trap had dug in clear to the bone and would not be gone in a day, but I could still work if it was wrapped tightly.

"Oh, thank goodness! I was so worried." Her frown vanished and was replaced with that glorious smile of hers that anointed me with her blessing. She was as disheveled as me, not that it mattered one whit. She would be lovely to me no matter what, even if she rolled around in the mud.

"I hear a helicopter," she said, looking up at the sky.

"Sounds like the cavalry has arrived."

"I called Lachlan last night. It must be him."

"You called my family home?" That surprised me.

"I called Skye first to get the number. Then talked with Lachlan. He said to wait for him, but I couldn't, I had to find you."

"Thank you for saving me."

"Well, you saved me first," she said in a teasing tone, and I knew for certain it was going to be all right. She'd made peace with who I was. We'd find our way through the last of the labyrinth.

"I want to be as strong as you," she mused, looking thoughtful.

"You managed to open the jaws of that steel trap. You're no slouch, angel."

"I want to be like you."

"Do you mean it? You want to have a second nature? Be able to shift?"

She nodded, her expression one of resolve. "Yes. Then we can be together without penalty."

"I would leave my clan, go it alone with you, if that was what you really wanted?" I suggested, not liking the strain in my voice. It pained me to the core, thoughts of leaving my family behind, but I would do it for Justine. Only for my angel would I contemplate such a thing.

"I would *never* ask such a thing of you. You have a history to preserve. A family who loves you. It makes more sense for us this way. How soon can we do it?"

Her eagerness touched me. She was all in. And she had never looked more beautiful or more alive.

"Let's wait until the shoot is concluded. You'll need time off and time is something we don't have to spare right now."

"Fine. But as soon as the final scene is concluded and not a second more."

Her eagerness touched me.

Then my brother was suddenly upon us.

"Logan! Are you okay?" Lachlan hugged me to his broad chest, a worried expression darkening his face. He was accompanied by our grandmother.

"I'm going to be fine. Just a bit banged up. My wife-to-be rescued me. This is Professor Justine Bell. Justine, my brother Lachlan and my grandmother, The Creig."

My grandmother frowned at Justine.

"What have you done to my grandson?" she asked, standing strong, the true matriarch evident in her stern expression and upright posture. Oh boy, she would not make this easy for my angel. How often had us three brothers been brought to task by her growing up? She had to be strong—the three of us were a handful. But she cared, if sometimes too much, and it was her way of communicating it. We were all grown up now and didn't need defending, but she was who she was and we all loved her for it. *After all, we are wolves.*

"I'm sorry. I didn't know, but I found him. I went into the desert to find Logan, to bring him home," Justine said, her eyes wide.

"Grandmother, Justine came for me. Don't blame her," I said.

The Creig's lips firmed into a tight line and I knew we hadn't heard the end of it.

"You're naked," Lachlan said, shaking his head with a chuckle, taking the heat off the situation. "What the hell happened?"

"Let's go inside and I'll fill you in," I said.

Chapter Twenty-Six

Hunter's moon, five weeks later
Justine

The last day of the shoot went well. After we wrapped up filming today, I was headed to Scotland with Logan to meet the clan at Castle Creigbourne. I glanced in the mirror. Skye had just completed his magic with my makeup and I took a moment to enjoy the glowing woman who stared back at me. *That's what sex a few times a day does for one's skin.* How had five weeks sped by so quickly? I shook my head. I knew how. So much had happened. But not as much as would occur tonight.

Am I ready for this? No going back once I crossed the line. I had to admit, I was a bit shaky.

"All set?" Valerie asked. She popped her head in the door, her eyes filled with anticipation of a level I had not seen her express before.

"Everything okay?" I asked.

"Of course. Just an exciting day with a crew party later to enjoy. Logan's even hired a big band with a major name. I don't know him. Michael something or other."

"Oh, girlfriend! How could you not know who that is?" Skye sounded scandalized, rolling his eyes with great glee when I glanced his way. "I'll give you a clue. His sound is fabulous. The Frank Sinatra of our generation!"

Valerie just shrugged. "No time for guessing. They're waiting for you on set."

I gave Skye an air kiss—he'd shoot me if I ruined his makeup—and followed the head writer from the trailer.

"So, you received the new lines last night?"

I nodded. "My ex is going to propose marriage, wanting me to run away with him to a private island with the money, but I turn him down, not wanting to spend my life in exile. Kind of sad. Logan's sure about this?"

"Yes, your character doesn't agree with his mission of getting revenge against the casino owner. She's upset that he hasn't really changed while she has. She wants the white picket fence and the golden retriever, not spend her life running from the law. She's grown."

"So, the heist is successful but he loses the girl. Guess crime doesn't pay."

"Exactly. Lovers pay or the loot is lost. There has to be a cost to crime."

We'd reached the set now, and I waited for my cue.

With the camera rolling, I stepped into character, the lines flowing out of my mouth as if I were born to it. Each day of acting had gone easier for me until now it was second nature. It didn't hurt that I had my own private mentor in Logan.

The scene unfolded, culminating in my final words. Tears were shed by most in attendance when I turned down the hero's marriage proposal. A touching moment captured for posterity.

Then Logan jumped down off the dolly and approached me as the crew broke into spontaneous applause.

"You won't marry him, but I hope you will say yes to me?" He bent down and got onto one knee, his ankle well healed now and no hindrance on set or in bed. That I could attest to. He held out a midnight-blue box in my direction, his heart in his eyes as we locked glances.

"Will you, Justine Katherine Bell, bless me with the honor of becoming my wife?"

My smile wreathed my face. "Yes! I most certainly will, Logan Johnathan Creig."

He opened the box. I held my hand out and he slipped the gorgeous antique thistle ring on my hand. *A perfect fit.*

"This is my great-grandmother's. She wore it for sixty-one years and fifty-five days. I know she's smiling down at us today, blessing us with the same longevity."

I loved the sound of that. A lifetime spent with this exciting and creative man could never be enough. We embraced to a thunderous round of applause.

"What say we slip out early on the party and head for the desert? Our plane doesn't leave until midnight," Logan whispered in my ear. "Plus, I'm the boss — they'll wait for us."

My heart beat faster as I thought about what was going to happen. "Yes, let's do that."

We stayed just long enough to say our goodbyes and promise another cast party on the anniversary date next year before hurrying away to valet parking.

Logan assisted me into the passenger seat of a sleek black Mercedes convertible and powered the top down, allowing the warm desert air to caress our skin.

"A Lamborghini *and* a Mercedes?" she teased.

"I wanted us to be together under the stars tonight and the red flash doesn't have that option," I explained with a wide grin. "I'm taking us to the Luceres estate. Cristaldo has offered his private land for our use tonight."

"That's good of him, considering it's a full moon. Surely others will want to make use of it?" I reached across the console and rubbed my hand up and down Logan's forearm. He'd rolled up his shirt sleeves and the bare, golden skin enticed me.

"Keep that up and we won't make it all the way there," he teased, his green eyes glancing my way and flashing brighter in warning.

I reached up and began to remove the pins from my upswept hairdo that had been decided on for that final scene, to show the character I was playing more in control when she rejected the hero. It felt good to let the long strands flow in the wind. Free.

"I've also taken the precaution of having the Lupus Sanguis Chalice with us in case you need assistance."

"That was thoughtful," I said, chewing on my thumbnail.

"I should warn you, each change is different. Some can shift right away, whereas with others, it can take many moons if at all. But the chalice is our saving grace. Before it was found in Alaska by the Luceres twins, well, suffice to say it was harder times."

"I believe what is meant to be will be. Knowing you has enhanced my philosophy. I think that far more exists on planet Earth than meets the eye." In Scotland, I'd be reunited with the Infinity Egg. So much promise for the future, it was mind-boggling. Would it lead to all humans knowing of our existence one day? Only time would tell.

"Good. Belief is an important consideration."

In short order, we turned onto the Luceres estate, the mansion and expanded wings coming into view under the starry night sky and reminding me of a beautiful famous painting.

"Let's do this outside, under the stars," I said.

"That's not what I planned."

"But it's far more romantic," I urged, turning my new engagement ring around and around on my finger. It felt so right, so welcomed, so promising. *Please be my talisman for tonight and assist me to become a wolf like Logan.*

"Okay, if that's what you want."

"It is."

We parked turned away from the lights of the mansion, to let the moon and stars be our guide.

Logan helped me out, then pulled a blanket from the trunk. We walked arm-in-arm down a path that led deeper onto the vast acreage. When we came to an amazing Joshua tree, he looked at me and I nodded.

"The perfect place."

He laid the thick cover on the ground. We embraced and he kissed me, his lips passionate, *seeking* as he laid me down. His scent and heat flowed into me, the sense of wonder tipping me into that incredible place where nothing else on earth existed except for us.

"I need you inside me, Logan, now!"

He tore off my underwear and grabbed me by the hips, driving himself in and out of me in long and oh-so-satisfying strokes. His cock rubbed hard against my clit and I gushed with wetness, easing the way. He pulled down my bra and sucked one breast while teasing the other with his fingers. He drew tightly on a nipple and my pussy clenched harder, desperate for release from this exquisite agony.

"Your cock was made for me," I said, breathless. I was so swollen that I had to come, to ease the throb. It was all I knew. All I could feel. I was out of control and sobbing my need aloud, gripping him harder to push him over the edge with me.

"This pussy is mine."

I struggled to meet his every thrust, grinding against him.

"Make me all yours, sir," I said, my need for release taking over. The connection was raw between us, overwhelming in its intensity. These past few weeks had only seen it grow stronger.

"Surrender to me," he growled.

"I want you. Mark me. Claim me." I knew the power of the words, because his expression turned to one of rapture and his green eyes smoldered.

With a hard thrust, he pushed into me, seating himself fully, every inch filling me completely. My breath seized. He rocked into me in a frenzy, grabbing at my hips and pulling me closer, my thighs wrapped around his hips.

I moaned, his wide girth sliding in and out in increasingly rapid strokes, our bodies slick with passion. His shaft thickened and lengthened beyond belief, pushing me to the limits. I rippled with involuntary spasms, my muscles clenching around the invasion. A climax shot through my system. But it wasn't enough. Not nearly enough. My body became hotter, my senses maddened.

He destroyed me. Powerful, deep thrusts filled me, such exquisite pleasure that I could scarcely hold on. Stars exploded behind my tightly closed eyes, brighter than the ones overhead in the night sky and I dimly heard myself sobbing with ecstasy.

The sense of being stretched grew stronger, wilder, and an urge to be filled beyond my limit allowed it to happen. The knotting. I knew when we locked together, our bodies becoming one, that it was everything. There could be no holding back.

"Ready?"

"Oh yes!"

There came a sharp pain in my shoulder that was followed by a soothing tongue when licked the spot, calming the nerves.

"It is done. I promise to be true to you and no other. To keep you safe and protected. To be only with you." His raw honesty and courage filled me to the brim, my eyes filling with tears. We were joined. Forever Mates. Spent, we lay side by side, proof of our passion scenting the night.

"I love you, Logan."

A sudden eruption began deep inside me, a sense of my body coming apart in a new way. Not from passion, but from another source. A bright light surrounded us.

Logan gasped aloud.

"You are a wolf, my angel."

He shifted then. We stood and stretched our limbs.

"Come, run with me."

His words filled my mind with promise.

"Race you," I teased. The next few minutes were as unbelievable as our lovemaking as we loped across the land, the night filling us to overflowing with its enchantment.

Good to be wolf.

And good to have shared everything with Logan now. All the events about those horrible characters that belonged to that strange cult-like group, Creation's Witnesses, including finding out that they had tossed my note about needing a bodyguard into the trash. Of course Logan had been angry at first, making me promise to never do that again. To never keep anything from him. And the Eternity Egg was safe and sound and I would soon have my hands on it again when we headed to Castle Creigbourne. *First order of business, find out all I can about real angels.* Logan had promised me all the time I could want or need with the amazing artifact. A whole world was opening up for me. A world of magic, a world of discovery and most importantly, a world of love.

So much had happened in my life these past few weeks. I had been on a journey few people could imagine. One that I was now appreciative of as I needed to learn another way. I had left the old Justine, the one who pushed away any opportunity for love thinking heartbreak would certainly ensue, only to discover one could have it all if they were willing to take the chance.

I was willing, in the end, and I was grateful and humbled that I had seen the light in time, even managing to lose my phobias along the way. *No self-respecting she-wolf can be afraid of anything, right?*

Now, my life was the best it could be. Me and Logan to the end. I was even going to take a hiatus from teaching for a year. Oh, and maybe hear the pitter-patter of tiny feet in the near future. Because, truth be known, I had something to tell Logan soon or be accused of keeping another secret from him…

All Hallows' Harem:
All Hallows' Bride
January Bain

Coming October 2023

Excerpt

I shut the book in disgust, snorting in annoyance at the romance story that had fulfilled its promise of happy-ever-after but left me feeling empty and cross. *Happy ever after. Yeah, right. Like that ever happens. Well, not to me anyway.* I frowned. A sweet romance was usually all that I needed to set me on the right path on a normal day, but this morning, it hadn't worked.

Maybe a darker romance was needed? Something so out of bounds that it freed me from, well, me? Because according to recent intel gained through bitter experience, I was *not* living up to my fun name. I was Lola in name only.

It didn't help that the rain that crept down my bookstore window and obscured the view of the street hadn't let up since I'd arrived this morning, giving me a bad case of the walking blues. Oh, and that being dumped by my boyfriend of two years last month wasn't enough. Or the fact he'd been cheating on me with my best friend. Now I was being asked to haul my ass all the way to Castle Creigbourne tomorrow to answer a summons.

That, I can promise, is not going to end well for yours truly. And here I thought I was out of sight, out of mind, the safest place to be as a poor relation from the sticks with a price on her head. Being gifted my own bookstore came with conditions, meaning my butt was on the line for a future favor.

And speaking of people letting me down, where was Serena? My one and only employee was late. Again. Okay, she didn't love Lola's Books & Mortar as much as me, but being on time for once would be a boon. But that got me right back to thinking and worrying about what the famous Highland Heathens Creig clan were going to demand of me. I owed them. Big-time.

In seeming answer to my question, the door opened, letting in the freezing draft of a colder-than-normal October. But instead of Serena racing in, apologizing for being late—something she'd gotten down to a fine art, by the way—it was him. The man who always came bearing surprises and secrets. My pulse speeded in anticipation though something about the man always made me shiver. What did he have for me today to add to my secret stash?

A tall, thin man in a fedora he kept pulled down low with only his pale face and a fringe of snowy hair exposed, he moved lightning-quick to join me at the counter, defying his age. His long black trench coat was covered in raindrops, as were his well-worn black leather dress shoes. I knew him only as Striker.

"Morning, Miss Lola," he said, his white even teeth barely showing as he gave me a tight-lipped smile.

"Mr. Striker," I said with a polite nod. He carried a small wrapped parcel tied with a length of coarse twine that my fingers twitched to unwrap. "What have you brought me today?"

"Ah, something of great note. I hope your coffers can support this addition," he said, his usual opening remark tinged with satisfaction.

"Business could be better," I said, making it clear I was not flush.

"Yes, can't it aways." He shrugged. "But this little gem is a one of a kind, I assure you."

I looked around the deserted shop, making certain no one else had come in and required assistance while I wasn't paying strict attention.

"You'd better come into the back." *Where in the heck is Serena?* She should have been here, making sure that any business, scant though it was, would be directed while I was occupied. Maybe I should lock the front door? But then even Serena wouldn't be able to enter and make at least a pretense of looking after things.

Much as I wanted to, I couldn't seem to fire the girl. I needed to grow a backbone, make my needs clearer to those around me who were trying to take advantage. Everyone thought I was loaded, thanks to my being related to the Creig clan, but business was down along with profits. And no way was I ever going to ask them for another red cent. Not until I paid off the loan that had begun Lola's Books & Mortar.

Striker nodded. "After you, Miss Lola."

He followed me down the aisle into my workroom, his footfalls so light as to be almost unnoticeable. The familiar scent of musty old tomes filled with ancient secrets gladdened my spirits, driving away my earlier doom and gloom. Mr. Striker's arrival, arresting and a bit scary as it always was when he showed up out of the blue a few times a year, promised a sensation of it being Christmas morn, with treasures nestled under the tree. Only these treasurers were deliciously dark and edgy, crafted by the unknown.

I gestured at the only free space on the long table that housed the paraphernalia for repairing old books and sundries. The shelving that the room was stuffed with contained many ancient artifacts that promised more than they provided. But the urge to think that maybe this one would be the one, the one item that would change something for the better and offer up an experience of great renown beckoned. I guess I was a sucker for such things, wishing always to understand the mysteries and secrets of the ancients. So much history was lost in the demands of day to day. "Shall we have a look?"

With pride, he laid the wrapped parcel on the wooden surface and stepped back, giving a courtly bow. "Please, after you, Miss Lola."

With trembling fingers, I worked on untying the sturdy string, fumbling in my excitement and wishing it would be considered good form to just cut it with a sharp pair of scissors. But I didn't want to appear gauche.

When it was done, I carefully peeled back the brown wrapping. I opened the midnight-blue cigar-sized box to reveal a small green glass vial with a filigree silver decoration.

"Very pretty. Perfume?"

"Not just any perfume, but something so special that it belies belief." Striker's eyes glittered with keen interest.

"Really?" Was he hawking a love potion? That was such a comedown from the usual exotic item he could entice me by. Plus, that ship had sailed, to borrow an old cliché.

"You're disappointed," he said, watching me carefully.

"No, it's very nice. Is it okay if I remove the stopper to check the scent?"

"Don't do that unless you have great need." His voice had changed with the warning, becoming harsher and with almost an echo to it.

"Okay. What's it for then?"

He smiled, revealing his teeth. "It can solve problems for those in dire circumstances. Like requiring to stay hidden."

Strange. But his words made my interest quicken. "What does it do? Mask scent or something?"

"Yes, at a cost."

My eyebrows rose. "What kind of cost?" Was he meaning the price he wanted for the strange item or the cost of using said item?

"Sorry I'm late! The rain caused an accident near my house and I had stop for ages because they closed traffic and I got stuck in the middle of things." Serena rushed in, a whirlwind of flying pink hair and dangling gold earrings that caught the overhead light as she tugged off her raincoat and hung it on a hook beside mine, showering the floor with rainwater that she wouldn't think to mop up.

"That's twice this month alone. Your street must be a lightning rod for accidents," I said.

Serena's rosebud lips turned down in a sulk before she realized I had company. "Oops, sorry for interrupting. Hello, Mr. Striker. What do you have for us today? Say, that's a bit of bling." She reached greedily for the bottle, but Striker intervened, slamming the hinged lid shut on the box and almost nipping her fingers in the process.

She stood there, looking rather pissed. "I'll catch you later, Lola. I have some news for you."

My employee loved to gossip. No doubt it was the ongoing saga of my ex-boyfriend and ex-girlfriend. No matter how many times I said I didn't care about them, still I seemed to find a moment to torture myself.

"Sorry about that. You were saying, Mr. Striker?"

He waved his hand like he was swatting at a bug. "The tag for this priceless item is rather steep, but as I was saying before the rude interruption, it would be well spent."

"More than for the Nightshade Web?" It had been a pricy box of cobwebs, but its promise of easing nightmares—or at least my memory of them—had worked after forking over a small fortune.

He'd come with some choice items over the past years, from the Book of the Dead that promised resurrection to a cure for the plague. I'd never tested them, as I liked to keep my karma in balance. Which apparently made me boring, according to my ex.

"I can let it go for the same amount."

I dithered. That was a lot of money. Hard-earned money and I still owed on the original loan. Not that the Creig clan would miss it. They were far richer than any on the Forbes List of—human—Billionaires. Shifters would never allow a list of their own kind. We kept to ourselves out of necessity and prudence. Our code of honor ran deep but our rules to live by were simple—*no exposing who we are to the world, and protect your own*. Standard fare for supernaturals. Striker was a werewolf just like me, so I had no problem dealing with him. He'd never shared what clan he was connected to, and I was too polite to ask.

"Can you come back tomorrow?"

"Tomorrow is too late. And once you purchase this, may I suggest you carry it wherever you go? Tie the vial around your neck and wear it as a talisman. It will bring you good luck."

That was a bit much. It wasn't even perfume.

"Humor an old man." His eyes bore into mine, like he wanted to say more.

"Fine. Okay, I might need to find a second job when I get back, but since it's one of a kind…"

"At least it will give you a running start."

What's that supposed to mean? "What does it purport to do?"

He gave a sly, rather surprising, strange smile. "It has an amazing ability to ward off the wearer's scent, making them impossible to track."

Taken aback by the intriguing information, I barely registered the sounds of arguing coming from the storefront. What was Serena up to? That the customer was always right was important to a floundering business. She'd better be behaving herself.

"I'll need to get your cash. Hold on." I hurried over to the corner and bent down to unlock the floor safe, careful to keep the combination hidden behind my hand, same as I did when using an ATM and I had to enter my pin number. I pulled out the required amount and shut the door firmly, ignoring how the pile within was dwindling.

"Here you go," I said, handing the stash of bills to him.

"Thank you," he said, touching his head in a respectful manner. "Until we meet again."

When I held out my hand to shake over the deal, he surprised me by kissing the back of it. "Don't underestimate yourself, Miss Lola. You have strong blood running through your veins that only needs a spark to ignite. Then watch out. The world will notice you and do your bidding. You're one of a kind and I see an amazing future for you. Find yourself and you can do anything. Even walk through walls."

I almost laughed at that comment. *Right.* No one did my bidding at the moment, preferring to take advantage of my good nature. And wasn't the correct expression *walk on water*? I just wanted to fall into stories and live my life through adventures that others took risks to go on. Was that wrong? *Maybe.* I was beginning to find being taken for granted a whole lot annoying of late. Serena thinking she had a job no matter what stunt she pulled. My best friend screwing my boyfriend.

That one hurt the most. Veracity had been my best friend since university and knew how much Riley meant to me. She could have any man, being sexy and gorgeous, so why did she take mine? A small voice in the back of my head said if he could be tempted to stray, he wasn't worth fighting for. Because truth be told, I did want a man so overwhelmed by my charms that he had to have me. *Is that too much to ask?*

The voices in the other room had grown louder.

"I'd better check on things."

"I bid you a good day, Miss Lola."

Striker left and I took a moment to admire my new acquisition before setting it safely on a shelf. *Okay.* No more dithering. I needed to restore peace.

About the Author

January Bain has wished on every falling star, every blown-out birthday candle and every coin thrown in a fountain to be a storyteller. To share the tales of high adventure, mysteries, and full-blown thrillers she has dreamed of all her life. The story you now have in your hands is the compilation of a lot of things manifesting itself for this special series. Hundreds of hours spent researching the unusual and the mundane have come together to create a series that features strong women who don't take life too seriously, wild adventures full of twists and unforeseen turns, and hot complicated men who aren't afraid to take risks. She can only hope the stories of her beloved Brass Ringers will capture your imagination as much as they did hers when she wrote them.

If you are looking for January Bain, you can find her hard at work every morning without fail in her office with two furry babies trying to prove who does a better job of guarding the doorway. And, of course, she's married to the most romantic man! Who once famously replied to her inquiry about buying fresh flowers for their home every week, "Give me one good reason why not?" Leaving her speechless and knocking her head against the proverbial wall for being so darn foolish. She loves flowers.

January loves to hear from readers. You can find her contact information, website details and author profile page at https://www.totallybound.com

Home of Erotic Romance

Sign up for our newsletter and find out about all our romance book releases, eBook sales and promotions, sneak peeks and FREE romance books!

Totally Bound Publishing books by January Bain

Brass Ring Sorority
Winning Casey
Chasing Lacey
Romancing Rebecca

TETRAD Group
Racing Peril
Racing the Tide
Racing the Whirlwind

Manitoba Tea & Tarot Mysteries
Magic, Mayhem & Murder
Movies, Moonlight & Magic
Moonshine, Magic & Murder

Sin City Wolf
Howl
Hunt
Honor
Hellfire

Sin City Kilts
Heart of Stone
Soul of Iron
Blood of Fire

Collections
A Little Bit Cupid: Lovestruck